THE GIRL HE LEFT BEHIND

OR

All Quiet in the Third Platoon

MARION HARGROVE

The Girl He Left Behind

or

ALL QUIET IN THE THIRD PLATOON

THE VIKING PRESS, NEW YORK, 1956

For Keith and Helen

Preface

A DOZEN YEARS AGO the Army of the United States was a boisterous, raucous, go-to-hell institution. Its voice was hoarse and loud, its tone was one of impersonal abusiveness, and its language was thick with four-letter words. Everything in its elaborate system seemed designed to augment the general chaos, its rules were made for circumvention, and its situation at any moment was considered normal only if it were all fouled up. The word "soldiering" itself had meaning and dignity then; it was a synonym for loafing and malingering.

Terrible things have happened to the Army in the intervening years. Beginning with the pressure of the Doolittle Board, which at the end of World War II studied ways of making the Army modern and enlightened, and coming down through the years under the leadership of numerous idealistic and public-relations-conscious men, it has become a quiet, stodgy, inoffensive old corporation, dedicated to efficiency, morality, and the importance of being Well-Liked.

The Army does not wish to be well-liked merely by veterans' pressure groups, and rampant American motherhood, and meddlesome old fence-menders in Congress. It wants to be well-liked even by the 1,296,387 men and women who comprise its membership. It is excruciatingly solicitous of the welfare of these people: muffling them against the weather, counting their calories, fussing over their civil rights, watching them anxiously for signs of discontent or boredom, and taking great pains to

7

see that no one hurts their feelings. It tries never to holler at them, even as groups, and it absolutely never singles them out for individual vituperation. It has so thoroughly discouraged uncouthness of language that that once noble military art has almost vanished. In all its daily life the Army of today is guided more by the chaplain than by the provost marshal.

The sour, snarling officer of yesterday has been relegated to a desk job in a back office. The howling, whip-cracking sergeant has been retired to civil life or shipped off to the Military Police. Corporals no longer give a man push-ups for punishment, because when the private does them the corporal is required to join him in the exercise. Second lieutenants are not as eager to receive salutes today, because officers returning salutes are supposed to smile pleasantly at the saluter and say, "Good morning!"—loud and clear and as if they really meant it.

To anyone who grew up with the Army half a generation ago, when a corporal's hand was heavy and a sergeant's voice could burn a timid recruit to a crisp, all this is a wistful thing to watch. One misses the profanity and the push-ups. One longs to hear again the simple homely sound of an institution shouting at an individual.

Why has the Army gone to hell?

A part of the blame must devolve upon ourselves and our times. This is the era of the efficiency expert, the psychologist, and the press agent, and the Army has adapted to it like practically everybody else.

A larger part is concerned with the type of people the Army has to work with. Most of the troops are in their teens, and few of them are career soldiers. They are the first peacetime citizen-army in the nation's history, and they are in for two years or three, depending on whether they are Selective Service men or Regulars. In the allotted time the Army must, in the interests of enduring national defense, mature their minds and muscles, their wits and their emotions, to whatever extent the public permits.

Fortunately for our story, there are still Army units that manage to remain a little behind the times. One of these is the Seventy-First Infantry, a training regiment at Fort Burnside, California, where voices are crisp and backs are straight and every boot shows spit and polish. This is because the regimental commander himself is belligerently old-fashioned and incurably military. When the colonel is shipped out or kicked upstairs, the Seventy-First will probably become like the others.

In Fox Company of the Seventy-First, the training company that provides the setting for most of this book, the average age of the trainees is eighteen. They are not draftees, since every man in the company volunteered himself into the spot he occupies.

According to the draft board, there are almost no actual draftees today. In the quiet little western community of Los Angeles the local tentacle of Selective Service maintains rather primly that it has not been obliged to coerce a man into the service for more than two years. The average young man, finishing high school, usually asks to have his name placed at the top of the draft list; he wants to get the whole thing over with as quickly as possible.

The record of the Los Angeles board was seriously threatened, for a while, by a blithe young man named Andrew J. Sheaffer. Mr. Sheaffer, a golden youth in his early twenties, had worked out a simple and graceful method for postponing his military career indefinitely. He intended to educate himself into the safe haven of middle age.

But, in the end, Andy volunteered like all the others.

Well, sort of.

THE GIRL HE LEFT BEHIND

OR

All Quiet in the Third Platoon

one

On a seemingly ordinary Thursday afternoon late last spring, Andrew J. Sheaffer came to the crossroads and knew it not. Even when he made the turn, changing the whole course of his carefree young life, he was unaware that anything had happened to him.

The crossroads was the intersection of Twenty-Sixth Street and San Vicente Boulevard in Santa Monica, and the turn he made was a left-hand turn in the path of a medium-sized truck. It was a calculated risk, a bluff such as Andy Sheaffer was accustomed to make at least six times every day.

The driver of the truck, whose aim it was to continue the truck's forward progress, was a quietly determined sort who did not relish being bluffed by smart-aleck kids. He not only had the unquestioned right of way; he had a larger and heavier vehicle than the one Andy was driving. He crumpled the fender of the little old Chevrolet convertible, paused long enough to ascertain whether Andy wanted to make anything of it, and continued the forward progress.

Andy Sheaffer got out of the automobile and inspected the remainder of the fender. Then he shrugged his shoulders, resumed his seat, and drove philosophically on. The only damage had been to his self-esteem. He had tried to bluff, and he had failed, and this was not an everyday occurrence in his life. Next to his charm, his bluff was the best weapon he possessed.

People of Andy Sheaffer's age and way of life are constantly banging up the fenders of automobiles, and few of them give the matter any more thought than Andy Sheaffer did. They differ from him, usually, in one respect: the fenders they bang up belong either to themselves or to their indulgent parents. The aged red convertible that Andy was driving on that decisive Thursday afternoon belonged to his current girl friend, one Susan Daniel, who had lent it to him while his own MG was having its lethal efficiency increased in a Santa Monica garage.

No eerie light appeared above the neighborhood of Twenty-Sixth and San Vicente. No great majestic thunder roared to tell the presence of the gods. Destiny had come, and done its work, and quietly gone away again. Andrew J. Sheaffer did likewise. No trouble stirred in his bright young eyes; no line of doubt or apprehension creased his forehead. So far as Andrew Sheaffer knew or cared, life was still his baby, and it was behaving for him as well as it always did.

Old people, such as you and I, concern ourselves too greatly over minor mishaps; perhaps we have too little faith in the essential equilibrium of life. The big, brown, good-looking kid in the red Chevrolet concerned himself not at all. A fender not his own had been a trifle smashed, but the world would still continue its monotonous rotation, and the sun would rise again tomorrow, as pink and cheery as it always was. The owner of the car, prim and responsible though she was, would pout a little and then be charmed out of her pique. The cost of the repairs would come to probably no more than forty dollars, and he would get the money from his mother. She would throw up her lovely young hands when he asked her for it, but he was her son, her ram lamb, and his foibles were laughable and his charm was great, and the hands would pat his handsome cheek and then reach for the checkbook.

His father, if he ever heard about the thing at all, would not be charmed. He would be quietly dry and disapproving, and he would get off a few well-phrased little philosophic

observations, and that would be the end of it. The elder
Sheaffer, like his wife, fitted well into Andrew's scheme of
things. He had decided long ago that perhaps nothing much
could ever be done with the boy, and he professed to have
stopped even trying to do anything with him. By Andrew
Sheaffer's standards, this made him an almost perfect father,
as fathers go.

Turning left on Wilshire Boulevard, Andy found himself
reflecting upon his father and his father's kind. In his mellow,
sophisticated way, the elder Sheaffer was still an aborigine, an
odd ball, a left-field square who persisted in playing it straight.
He had picked up the idea, back in the Ice Age, that life is
real, life is earnest; and he would carry this conviction with
him to the final curtain.

Life may be real, said Andy, but nowhere in the book does
it say that life has to be earnest. Looking at it that way, all
that you can hope to get is thick lenses. I wish I could tell
him, he said, and make him believe it, that there is no real
need to go splashing furiously through life; you can get just
as far, almost as fast, by turning on your back and floating.

Perhaps, though, it was not age that made his father splash
about. Even among Andy's own contemporaries there were
those who faced life with a straight face and drooping shoulders, kids who were as good as beaten before they ever started.

For example, the boys who had finished high school with
him. Most of them had clutched their sheepskins in their
earnest little hands and started out immediately for downtown
Los Angeles, turning themselves in to the draft-board officials.
This was not stupidity; it was ordinary panic. As a consequence,
large numbers of them were college freshmen now, when
actually they should be juniors, like himself.

But for the grace, he reflected, I could have panicked too.
I could have gone charging down there, full of dread and
eagerness, and begged them to shove a musket into my hands.

If I had, God knows, I might be out there right now in some Army camp in Arizona, with Richard Widmark telling me how little time he has to make a soldier of me.

You don't have to do things that way. All you have to do is to keep cool and keep smiling and keep your wits about you. I have had almost three pleasant years at the University-of-California-at-Los-Angeles, studying just hard enough to maintain the minimum academic level. I get my sunshine on the beach instead of on the drill field, and no one is really the loser—because any time the Army really needs me for a soldier, soldiering is not a hard profession or a slow one to pick up. Another year of liberal arts and generous leisure and then I can decide to go to law school. The months and the years drop off the calendar, and a man eventually reaches twenty-six, and then there's not a damned thing the Army can do to him.

He made another turn, into the street where Susan lived, and took a quick look at his watch. There was still some of the afternoon left. Perhaps, if he could get her quickly through the inevitable brouhaha about the fender, he could bring her home with him for a dip in the pool.

Susan's earnestness, unlike his father's, never bothered Andy at all. It seemed sometimes almost like a carry-over from childhood: the serious, frowning concentration of a three-year-old faced with a coloring book and a choice of crayons. It was funny in a sweet sort of way, or perhaps funny was not really the word for it. Perhaps the word was appealing.

One thing he had to give her: sober as she was at times, she seldom let it get in her way for very long. Any other girl half as responsible would have impressed Andy Sheaffer as a real cold-cut, a mothball. He would have taken one look at her, added up the tab, and broomed off quickly, leaving no forwarding address. Don't call us, kid; we'll call you.

Not Susan. Not to Andy. She was, in the stately vernacular of youth, a hot spook, and she would have had it made with him even if she had worn Sensible Shoes. She was in essence younger and handsomer and actually even gayer than he, and it would have been hard for him to set a pace that she could not match. In the important aspects of everyday life she was right in there with the group. She could handle a horse or a sailboat as easily as he; she could pick up a dance step even quicker; and she could beat him at gin or Scrabble at least two games out of five.

Her only flaw was that recurrent little earnestness, and, if this were treated with patience and tolerance, she would undoubtedly get over it. Until then, it was no heavy cross. It made her seem small and feminine, and sometimes it boosted him and made him feel almost protective.

Andy parked the car in front of the house and took another look at the fender. Just about forty dollars, he figured.

Going up the front walk, he gave a shout, and Susan answered from the back yard. They met halfway, in the driveway beside the house, and she gave him a kiss on the nose. She took his hand as they walked toward the back yard.

"What did you do last night," she asked, "when the rest of us were cramming for exams?"

"I stayed at home and took care of my little silver-haired mother. Three games of Scrab, and I beat the socks off her all three times."

"That's very impressive," she said. She sat down on the back steps, and he sank down beside her.

"Not really," he said. "The old man was playing too. I got to play both my new words."

"Not that Arabic one!" said Susan.

"In the second game. It was practically the last time around, and there I sat with the Q in my hand, and you could see that Madeline had practically nothing. She played AD down in the corner—and that's the sort of word she always has to fight Pop for—and when I put the Q in front of it and the I behind it I thought the roof was going to cave in. Q-A-D-I, with a triple-letter score on the Q!"

"If I'd been your mother—God forbid—I would have gone for your jugular."

"It was the old man who really frosted," said Andy. " 'Queigh-dye?' he says. 'What the hell kind of word is queigh-dye?' 'Not queigh-dye, Father,' I told him. 'It's kah-dee, like there was an umlaut over the A.' He started hollering for the dictionary, and I jumped to fetch the big Webster. He was absolutely purple when he found the word blinking back at him."

"I wouldn't have accepted it," said Susan. "What did your mother say?"

"She was tickled. She never suspected there was a 'q' word that didn't need a u. She didn't get frosted until the next time, when she played AX and I put the z in front of it."

"Spell 'weird,' " said Susan.

"Ho ho ho," said Andy.

"Just for the heck of it," she said. "Spell 'weird.' "

"Look, Edgar," said Andy. "You take the straight lines. I'll handle the jokes."

"Speaking of handling," she said, "would you remove your hot hands from under my rib cage? I'm awfully ticklish there, as you very well know."

"Ticklishness," he said, tickling her lightly, "is a manifestation of your whole endopsychic censorship."

"Stop it, you fool!" she shrieked. "You want my mother to come out?"

"What are we doing tonight?" he said suddenly, seriously. "I know a drive-in theater with an awfully dull picture. It's going to be a glorious evening for necking in open cars."

She laughed. "Go find someone else for your open cars, at least until exams are over."

"You're going to be *studying?* *Again?*"

"That's what we all do, we dull ones. It isn't as grueling as you think. Why don't you try it sometime?"

"Because," said he, "I'm not an intellectual snob. I know my place—the very bottom of the upper half of my class. That keeps the draft board happy without exciting envy and jealousy among my schoolmates."

"Andy," she said, "if you keep talking like that—all this draft-dodger routine—people are going to start believing you. It's very nice and charming as long as it's a gag, but not everybody knows it's a gag."

"Yes, Mother," he said.

She carefully changed the subject. "Did you get squared away at the garage?"

"Well," said Andy, "I got squared away for my car, but not for yours."

"For mine!" she said, jumping to her feet. "What have you done to my car?"

"Completely smashed," he said. "Straight through the bridge rail. A sheer drop of fifty feet. Plummeting down, like a stricken bird, to the dry, hard, unyielding concrete bed of the Los Angeles River. Hastily donning my jumpsack, I bailed out at angels thirty and watched the gallant little ship crash in flames below me."

"Andy," she said, "I'm not asking. I'm demanding. Where is my car?"

"It's out front," he said. "I told them I'd return the tow truck in the morning."

She marched off around the house, and Andy followed her, tickled by her belligerent anxiety. She looked at the fender, walked around to the side of the car, and looked at it again. Then she let out a sigh that sounded as if she had been holding her breath for a long time.

He took her hand and led her back to where they had been

sitting before. "I'm very sorry it happened, angel. You won't believe me, but I am."

"I believe you," she said. "At least, in a way I do."

"I'll take it over tomorrow, and have it patched up and hammered out so that you wouldn't even know anything had happened to it."

"How did it happen?" she asked.

"I tried to browbeat a truckdriver," said Andy, "and he just wasn't a timorous type. Well, that's the way the ball bounces."

"He could have killed you," said Susan, "and wrecked my car besides. Is it going to cost an awful lot to fix?"

"Maybe forty bucks," said Andy. "Maybe fifty. But them's the vicissitudes. Easy come, easy go."

"Andy, that's awful," she said, genuinely concerned. "You don't have that kind of money to throw around. You don't even have a job."

"What do I need with a job?" said Andy, smoothing out the wrinkle in her forehead. "I have guardian angels hovering about me. I am fed by the ravens. What raven is going to get an ulcer over forty bucks?"

The hand and arm under his disengaged themselves, and Susan sat up straight. "I'm very serious about this," she said. "Don't be charming, and don't be evasive. Where are you going to get the money?"

"I'll think about it later," he said. "Why should you sit around screaming about forty bucks? It's just a handful of green stamps."

"You don't have that many green stamps."

"I know people who *do*."

"Everything is very funny to you," she said. "When you say, 'Easy come, easy go,' you really mean it, don't you? Who's going to give you forty dollars?"

Andy merely grinned at her show of emotion.

"Your mother?" she said.

"Stop it," said Andy. "Give us a great big smile."

"*Is* it your mother?"

"Come on," said Andy. "I'll buy you a soda."

"No, thanks," she said, standing up again. "It's getting cool. I think I'll go in." Andy looked at her in mild puzzlement. "Will you excuse me?"

"Reluctantly," said Andy. "Every time we say good-by, I die a little."

After she had gone into the house, he still sat there for a while, with a quizzical smile playing over his face. There she goes again, he said to himself. There is a weird streak of something or other in this dear little creature, but that's what makes them interesting.

❖

"Not at the moment," said Madeline Sheaffer. "I was completely cleaned out at canasta yesterday, but I suppose I can get it from your father. Whatever on earth do you need fifty dollars for?"

She was sitting at her elaborate dressing table, buffing her fingernails. Andy sat, half recumbent, on the corner of her bed. He lit a cigarette and placed it in her mouth.

"I had a teensy little automobile accident, and it wasn't my car. It's a very awkward feeling."

"Don't I know," said Madeline. "Who was foolish enough to lend you an automobile this time?"

"The one and only."

"That's vague enough," she said.

"Susan, Mother. You remember Susan?"

"I remember the car. Mangy old red convertible, isn't that the one? I must say, *she*'s been around a long time."

"Could I have the fifty by afternoon?"

She laid down the buffer and extricated the cigarette from between her lips. "Sweetie," she said, "I'm certainly not going to tackle him while he's sitting down there frowning over the morning paper. These things have to be timed perfectly."

"The only thing, Mother—"

"He's probably at this very moment reading a speech of Vice-President Nixon, and you know perfectly well what that does to his disposition."

"I need it this afternoon, Mother," he said. "It's a sacred obligation."

"Then be a dear sweet lad and leave me alone," said Madeline. "I'll get it for you. I always do, don't I?"

❖

In the afternoon, back from school, Andy found the money waiting for him under the big ashtray on his bedside table. He stuffed it, still in the envelope, into his shirt pocket and lightheartedly set out afoot to pick up the little old red convertible at Susan's house.

She was not at home, and neither was the car. Her mother, a hesitant-looking creature who was forever nervously patting her hair into place, met him at the door and let him into the living room, as if she could not think of anything else to do with him.

"Oh yes," she said, "the car went off to the garage this morning, bright and early. Susan had them send a man over to pick it up. Said there was no reason to trouble you about it, and that's the way she does things."

"Oh," said Andy, unexpectedly disconcerted.

"Yes," said Mrs. Daniel for no apparent reason.

"Not back from school yet, I suppose," said Andy.

"Well, she was in and out—you know how she is. She said something about going over to some girl friend's house. They're cramming for an examination, I think she said. Chaucer, or one of those people. She told me the girl's name, but you know how I am about remembering that sort of thing."

"Yes, ma'am," said Andy.

"I've never been any good at all at remembering that sort of thing. And so many of them."

"Yes, ma'am." The realization that he was inwardly irritated served to irritate him even more, but he managed to look as pleasant and sincere as always. This creature's dialogue, he said to himself, is like something out of "Dragnet." Is that why I keep saying "Yes-ma'am" to her?

"You'd probably like a beer or something," said Mrs. Daniel. "Or there's soft drinks too in the icebox."

"Thank you, no," he said. "Will you tell her I'll see her this evening?"

"I knew there was something," said Mrs. Daniel. "Susan said that if you called or anything, she's probably going to be studying so late that you'd better not depend on this evening."

"Oh," he said again, feeling a little foolish that that was the best he could manage.

"Yes," said Mrs. Daniel.

"Would you give her this?" he said, handing her the envelope from his shirt pocket. "I promised to drop it off."

Mrs. Daniel took the envelope, looked at it with vague discomfort, as if she knew what was in it, and foolishly patted her back hair again. He said his good-bys, and found his way back out of the house, and walked home slower than he had come.

Technical difficulties somewhere west of Denver, he said as he rounded the corner. I'm getting an awfully weak signal.

❖

Arthur Sheaffer's mood at dinner was mellow and benign. His shaggy eyebrows rode high, furrowing his forehead all the way up to where his hairline must once have reached, and his warm brown eyes crinkled and twinkled behind the heavy frames of his glasses. Even the tips of his bow tie seemed alert and perky.

He gave a gay and courtly little nod to his wife, and bestowed upon his son a look that was almost beaming. "The clear, bright faces of youth," he said. "Mrs. Sheaffer, you look uncommonly radiant this evening. Andrew, the mustard, please."

"Why are you so chipper in the evening, and so unbearable at breakfast?" Madeline asked him.

"Because, in the morning, I am not surrounded by the clean-cut, loving faces of my family. Because, in the morning, the whole world is new and I am older than ever."

"God help us," said Madeline. "The manic phase is upon him."

"I find myself increasingly reluctant to escort you out into society," said Arthur. "People look at you—immediately, of course—and then they look at me, and they say to themselves: Lecherous old devil. Sugar daddy. Old enough to be her father."

"Really, Arthur," she said, the vanity throbbing in her voice. "Such wild, extravagant—"

"Not at all, my dear," he said, gaily waggling his fork at her. "You look like a young girl of thirty-five—no, thirty-three—who takes good care of her looks. If I did not know you, I would never guess that you were—"

"We can get along without all that," said Madeline. "Eat your dinner."

He turned to his son, who was silently picking at his food. "And to come to dinner and find you here! Really, Andrew, my cup runneth over. It isn't every evening that we get a treat like this."

"Mother," said Andrew, "take his temperature." He shook his head and methodically resumed eating.

"Madeline," said Arthur, "did you notice when he lifted his face out of the plate? He has a little worried look about him. I've never seen such a thing before. I must say, Andrew, it's really quite becoming."

"Arthur," said Madeline. "Eat. You haven't stopped talking since the minute you sat down at this table."

"I can't imagine what a person like him could possibly find to worry about. I'm quite intrigued. I hadn't thought him capable of burrowing down to that emotional level. It heartens me."

"Mother!" said Andy.

"It can't be work," his father said serenely, "because he hasn't any work. It can't be responsibility, because that's beyond his ken. Perk up, Andrew. I'm sure it's something purely somatic."

"Leave him alone," said Madeline. "He's just having trouble with some girl."

"Indeed?" said Arthur, genuinely intrigued. "I couldn't be happier for him. It must be a novel and exciting experience."

"Mother," said Andrew, "will you ask him please to get up off me? I can't stand it when he's droll."

"I'll be good," said Arthur. "Why is the girl giving you trouble?"

"Because," said Madeline, "she's just a nasty, disagreeable girl. Now I think we should drop the subject."

"Which girl is it?"

"The Daniel girl. Eat your dinner."

"Nasty?" said Arthur. "Disagreeable? Nonsense. She's an utterly enchanting girl. She's delightful. She's the only nice one he's had around here. What are the two of you fighting about?"

Andy laid down his fork. "Snooping, prying, meddlesome old man," he said. "Mother, he is inexcusable."

"Well," said Arthur, smiling happily, "I shall be very curious to see how it all turns out."

❖

Finally, on Sunday, Andy managed to get through to her. She was in the back yard, sitting in a deck chair with an unopened book beside her. The only other chair nearby faced hers from a distance of at least five feet.

Unerring instinct told him not even to kiss her cheek. He sat down in the vacant chair and grinned at her. It was his youngest, most boyish, most winning grin, one that on ordinary occasions could cut through even his father's knowing crustiness. This time it fell flat and lay there.

"What's the rap?" he asked her.

"Rap?" she said. "I'm afraid I don't know what you mean, Andy."

"I seem to be sitting here in Coventry," he said, "and you sit there looking like early Olivia De Havilland, and no bill of particulars. You could at least tell me what the hell I've done."

"You haven't done anything, Andy. It's just—I don't know."

"Then what are you waving the bloody shirt for?"

"I'm not waving the bloody shirt, Andy."

Both of them were silent for an awkward half-minute.

"If it's about the car, I said I'm sorry, and I am. It never should have happened, and—"

"The car's all fixed now," she said. "Let's forget it."

"So it's not the car," he said. "So it's something else. What?"

"Andy, it's nothing. What are you trying to do?"

"Just get the argument started right, so we can get through it and wrap it up."

She had nothing to say. He fumbled through his pockets, looking for cigarettes, and found that he had none. "May I have a birdwood?" he asked her. "I seem to be clean."

She handed him the cigarettes. He lighted one, and remembered to give the others back to her.

"Flutterbum," he said as winningly as he could, "drop the other shoe, will you? You're being weird and sticky, and we might as well know why."

She pulled her lower lip between her teeth and looked away. "That's the whole problem, Andy. I'm just weird and sticky, and you're not, and that's all there is to it."

Beside his chair someone had left an old croquet ball. He picked it up, studied it carefully, and set it down again.

"I'm not your type," she said suddenly.

"That's a gasser," said Andy. "That's *really* a gasser."

"Let me say it while I have it straight. It's taken me a long time to get it straight. We've had some wonderful times, for you're very good at fun and games, Andy, but sometimes I keep thinking that that's all we'll ever have—fun and games. Everything with you is cotton candy, and that's just not a staple."

"This is silly," said Andy.

"I like to have fun," she said. "I like to play. But sometimes when we're playing I get a little chill in my stomach—and I say to myself: Susan, it's getting late. The trouble with me, Andy, is that when you really get down to it, I'm a stick, a clod, a wet rag."

Andy groped for her hand, but she pulled it away. "Kid," he said, "you've really got your head in a bag."

"I know," she said. "That's what I'm talking about. You'll never have your head in a bag. You're smooth and slick and quick on your feet, and nothing is ever going to touch you. You need fifty dollars, and there's a raven to give it to you. You see trouble coming, and you know all the little exits to duck it. You want to make C in a course at school, so you read the book once and close it for the rest of the semester. Life will never whip you, because life will never get its hands on you."

"So?" said Andy.

She shrugged unhappily. "I'm just not like that. I'm a real square. I can dance as late as anyone else, but I still rinse my nylons the minute I take them off. I even put money in a savings account. And when I see trouble coming—well, most of the time, anyway—I have a compulsion to meet it head-on."

"Why?" said Andy, genuinely curious.

"I guess it's a personality defect. My grandfather used to have a saying—he spent his whole life in the Army, and I guess he picked it up there. He used to say, 'If it doesn't hurt, you're not doing it right.' He didn't mean exactly that. I think he meant that if it doesn't cost anything, it isn't worth anything."

"That's very solemn and impressive," said Andy. "What's the payoff?"

"There isn't any payoff, I guess. It's just what they call a Slice of Life."

"What are we doing this evening?"

"I'm going out to dinner with my parents."

"Tomorrow?"

"Studying."

"And after that?"

She looked him straight in the eyes, but her lower lip quivered before she could speak. "I'm going away for the summer. I'm going to visit my grandmother."

"Grandmother!" he said, exasperated by now. "Lover! A fight's a fight, but let's not get stuck in the trenches!"

"It's not a fight, Andy. It's just a wrong number, and I'm the one who goofed." He wanted to say something, but she forged ahead. "I've had a wonderful time, and I love you very much, and I'm dreadfully, dreadfully sorry!" With that, she bounded out of her chair, kissed him before he knew what was happening, and dashed across the lawn to the house.

She was crying when she reached the back door, and she had an awkward time opening it, and when she was inside, it slammed unhappily behind her.

Andy still sat in the deck chair, trying to gather the pieces.

❖

Actually, that was about all there was to it. When the back door slammed behind Susan Daniel the finger of fate had already done its work. All that remained were a few loose ends for Andy Sheaffer himself to tie up.

One thing must be said for Andy Sheaffer. The world, and

Susan, and everything but the finger of fate, had underestimated him. He could be touched. He was, for at least that decisive moment, more than touched. It would be hard to say what hit him—anger or hurt or merely confusion at finding that this time he himself was the jetsam on the beach—but whatever hit him clobbered him.

Before another Sunday came around he had stumbled into the second phase. He had missed one examination and flunked two others. The former schoolboy, Classification 1-SC, was now a man, 1-A.

Not that simply, and not that quickly. He went down to the draft board, just to check, and the man there gave him the schedule.

First the university would send in his Form 109, the report of his scholastic rating, and it would be August before the 109s were processed. A Form 110 would be sent to him, advising him of his new classification. Then a Form 123 would invite him to report for a physical examination, after which nothing much would happen for perhaps three months.

Around Christmas he could expect Form DD 62—Certificate of Acceptability. This would be followed, precisely three weeks later, by SSS 252—The President of the United States to Andrew J. Sheaffer, Greeting.

"That will make you," said the Selective Service man, "our first involuntary draftee in twenty-six months."

"The hell it will," said Andy. "I'm volunteering!"

And so he did. He ran away from home, confident that they would all be sorry when he was gone.

❖

The elder Sheaffer came home in the middle of the afternoon— not because it was a beautiful day, or because he had caught up with his work, but because he simply could not get any work done. If he were going to pace, and jump when the telephone rang, he might as well do it at home, with a drink in his hand. The publishing business could go to hell just as easily without him.

He found his wife sitting in the middle of the living-room floor, looking very small and dejected and frightened.

"What on earth are you crying about?" said Arthur Sheaffer. "There's nothing to cry about."

"He looked so miserable, leaving to go downtown this morning. And in a taxicab. He wouldn't even let me take him downtown."

"That's understandable, I think," said Arthur.

"And you!" she said. "You should be thoroughly ashamed of yourself! You're to blame as much as anybody else for the whole thing. All of you getting him so worked up that he didn't even know what he was doing. First that utterly horrible girl, throwing him over just before exam week, and in such an utterly nasty way. And then you, sitting around cackling and goading him with that utterly despicable little sarcasm of yours, making it worse. Arthur, your conduct has been really shocking."

"Nonsense," he said gently. "He's been exposed to that utterly despicable little sarcasm all his life, and I'm sure he never hears a word of it. That's one of the most frustrating things about Andrew."

"You're actually glad to see him go!"

"Yes, dear," he said mildly.

"You've never understood him. You've never tried to."

"Madeline," he said, "I shall try as long as I live to understand him, and one day, God willing, I will. I am impatient with him, but only in one respect. I want to see him grow up one day, and this is the one thing he doesn't want to do. I think sometimes that it's the one thing *you* don't want. It heartens me to think of him, after all this time, a soldier in the Army. Maybe the Army can do for him what I haven't been able to do. Maybe the Army can help him to grow up."

Madeline's handkerchief hand dropped, and she gave him a look of cold fury. "Help him to grow up?" she said. "Do you know where he is right now?"

"Do *you?*"

"He's in a dingy, drafty waiting room on North Figueroa. They pulled and poked and tested him from eight this morning until two in the afternoon, and stamped him approved and swore him in. And now he's sitting there waiting to be thrown aboard a troop train or something. And while he's waiting, do you know what the Army has provided—for him and the others—to occupy their time and help them to grow up?"

"What, dear?"

"Comic books!"

two

THERE WAS ASTONISHINGLY little joking, except among the naked boys themselves, and theirs was the forced humor of bravado. There was none of the roughness that Andy had expected to find, as a matter of course, in everything connected with the service. The examination routine was deliberate, careful, and almost determinedly courteous.

The man ahead of him, he saw, was having his pulse counted. His name Andy had heard as Hanson, and he was older than most of the men in the line. He looked as if he were probably somewhere in his thirties.

The medic looked quizzically into the man's face. "The real article," he said. "A *voluntary* volunteer."

"How can you tell?" Hanson asked.

"Pulse," said the medic. "Draftees are numb; volunteers are nervous. Prior-service man?"

"World War Two," said Hanson. "Just coming back in."

"Couldn't be from hunger," said the medic.

"I couldn't say what it is," said Hanson. "Just homesick, I guess."

"Or crazy," said the medic.

"Or crazy," said Hanson.

When Andy had had his own pulse counted, and submitted six cubic centimeters of his blood for analysis, and demonstrated that he could distinguish one color from another, and had his hearing and his blood pressure checked, and assured the final physician that he was not addicted to narcotics or troubled by any problems that the Army should be troubled by, he was through.

So far, he said to himself, this is the longest day I have ever been through. He looked at the large clock on the wall. It said 9:45.

Back in the locker room with the others, he had barely had time to dress when one of the sergeants beckoned them all to follow him out again. "Let's go," said the sergeant. "Noon chow!"

No one paused to challenge the order or question the schedule. At ten o'clock in the morning they were sitting down quietly to lunch.

At ten forty-two they all lifted their right hands and repeated the words read by the lieutenant on the stage of the auditorium.

At ten forty-three they were all duly qualified and registered members of the Army of the United States.

In the waiting room—where no one bothered to tell them

what they were waiting for, if anything—Private Andrew J. Sheaffer found himself sitting next to a large old gentleman of perhaps twenty-six or twenty-seven, with a great round face and huge black-rimmed glasses that did little to hide the sharpness and the anger in the eyes behind them.

"Rape," said the large recruit, disgustedly throwing aside a comic book named *Archie*.

"Sheaffer," said Andy, taking his hand. "Andy Sheaffer."

"My name is not Rape," said the other, "and don't get people thinking it is. My name is Ransom Maguire, and I want to see my lawyer."

"Would you like us to draft him too?" said Andy.

"Don't be silly. He isn't even married."

"That takes care of that," said Andy.

"Sheaffer, never trust a woman."

"What have they done this time?"

"I took her for richer or poorer," said Maguire. "In sickness and in health. And, brother, did she take me! The wife of my bosom. The mother of my child."

"What did she do?"

"She went to Mexico," said Maguire, "on advice of counsel. She went for her freedom at the cost of mine. The divorce papers said she was a registered resident of Tijuana. That's a section of Pasadena I never heard of."

"It takes two to make a Mexican divorce," said Andy. "Why'd you give it to her?"

"I was conned," said Maguire. "Flimflammed. I thought I was getting *my* freedom. Now she is single and independently wealthy—division of community property, you know—and me? Old and poor and broken, and no longer the bona fide head of a household. What business is it of the government whether I have my own household or not?"

"It's like taxes," said Andy. "When you pick a winner at the track, the government goes with you to collect. It's the same way here. You won your freedom, and this is the government's cut of it."

"You're a brighty boy," said Maguire, "and a philosopher. You better stick with me to stay out of trouble."

"Find me a trouble," said Andy, "worse than the one I've got already."

A sergeant walked to the front of the room. "All right, you men!" he bellowed. "The following men have been dogeared for Fort Burnside, California. You've got three hours to take your excess gear home, and you will be in the south patio of Union Station at six-forty Pacific Standard Time, which is an hour later than you think it is. If you got any questions, you better be asking them now, because there's one thing we don't like in the Army, and that one thing is confusion."

Fort Burnside California, said Andy. Never heard of it. But then, as he was to learn later and gradually, there were a lot of things he had never heard of.

❖

Carleton, the extremely young- and pleasant-looking Negro kid in the corner seat opposite Andy, peered through the window, trying to read the signs outside as they passed them. "Best I can make out," he said cheerfully, "we're going through Burbank."

"That's a good place to be going through," said Maguire. "At this rate we'll be out of the city limits by this time tomorrow."

Hanson, the fourth man in the compartment, looked up from the orders he was studying and smiled. "You in a hurry, soldier?" he said.

Hanson, because of his age and prior service, had been appointed group leader for the trip north to Fort Burnside.

"Do me a favor," said Maguire. "Don't call me soldier till you have to. It gives me the creeps."

Andy gazed moodily down the aisle. In the end compartment two young men apparently of Mexican extraction sat apart from all the others, too full of dread to talk even to each other. In the second compartment a fat youth in a T-shirt searched his fingertips with his teeth, seemingly in the desperate hope of finding one last little shred of chewable nail. This one, Andy decided, was unquestionably the most nervous lad in the whole contingent. All day long, between attacks on his fingernails, he had been feverishly scratching himself.

From somewhere back in the fast-receding past, Andy suddenly remembered a lament of his father, who never scratched like the fat boy across the aisle, but often rubbed himself against the back of his chair. "The sensitive man of today," Arthur had said, "itches for a little less convenience and a little more comfort. My itch lies between my shoulder blades, easy and accessible; another man's is buried in his stomach. Each of us, Andrew—the dermal and the duodenal—takes his little pill and envies people like you."

It was difficult to realize that less than half an hour separated Andy from all of that: his father fussing at him, his mother fussing over him, and neither of them making much of a dent upon his durable hide. Standing in the patio in Union Station, both of them had looked older and smaller: Madeline, striving to be brave and gay, showed all her forty-seven years; and Arthur, strangely sober and thoughtful and devoid of his almost constant little twinkle, was all at once an elderly little man, bald and bent and sad-eyed. When the Navy's shore patrolmen appeared to take the recruits away to the train, Arthur had briefly hugged his son, a thing he had not done in years, and with great and touching dignity kissed him on the cheek.

Maguire's voice cut into Andy's thoughts. He was balefully

addressing himself to Carleton. "If all you can do at a time like this is to sit there grinning," he told the boy, "I'm going to revise my whole attitude toward you. What the hell have you got to grin about?"

Carleton merely grinned at him.

Hanson laughed. "Carleton," he said. "Tell me. How old are you?"

"Seventeen," said Carleton.

"Damned if you look it," said Hanson. "What brought you into the Army?"

"That's a long story," said Carleton. "I guess you'd say my mother brought me."

"That's a good way to start a story," said Maguire. "If I were still a big Hollywood agent, like I was yesterday, I could sell that one just on the strength of the opening."

"The way it was," said Carleton, "I was out of school, and I had a job in the chair factory, and the foreman he was pushing us, and I didn't like that. Then I was having a hard time finding a new job, and my mother didn't like me staying out late every night. So she just laid it down. She said, 'Henry,' she said, 'first thing you know you're going to be a juvenyle delinquent, running around with one of them rat packs. You want to go to the Army, or you want to go to reformatory?' So that's why I'm here."

"Your mother," said Maguire, "ran you into the Army to keep you off the streets?"

"My mother is a smart woman," said Carleton.

Hanson studied first his papers and then the boy's face. "If that's all she wanted, why didn't you just volunteer for the draft?"

"That's what I did," said Carleton. "Volunteered."

"No, sir," said Hanson. "According to the orders here, you enlisted. You're in the Regular Army, like me."

"What's the difference?" said Carleton.

"A year, son," said Hanson. "Regulars are in for three years. Draftees are in for two."

Carleton looked at Andy, who nodded confirmation. Then he cocked his head and thought for a while. "I sure wish," he said, "somebody had told me that back there."

"It would have saved a lot of time," said Maguire.

"Time I get out of the Army," said Carleton, "why, I'll be almost old enough to vote." He grinned again, savoring his predicament. "Ain't that a bite?"

A small contingent of men converged upon the compartment. "Hanson," said one of them, "there's a club car up front. Are we allowed to go to the club car?" He said it as if he fully expected to be forbidden.

"It's a public train," said Hanson. "Just don't order any liquor and don't do any gambling."

"No, sir," said the whole contingent.

"And don't spend the night up there," said Hanson. "We're going to be hopping off this train awful early in the morning."

"You guys want to come along?"

"I think I will," said Carleton. "See what a club car looks like. I've never been on a train before."

"It figures," said Hanson, when the others had gone. "This part of the country, they got two kinds of transportation—automobiles and airplanes."

Andy Sheaffer, moving into the vacated window seat, had a sudden realization and said nothing about it. He himself, the boy sophisticate, had never been on a train either.

❖

At three o'clock in the morning the streamliner paused at Esperanza long enough for two dozen young men to stumble out into the chilly air. No brass band blared upon the little platform. No welcoming committee was there—not even a

buck-bottom private with an Army truck. Hanson managed to
herd the little group together in some sort of double file,
slouching and sleepy; three or four of the men shivered unhappily in the short-sleeved sports shirts they had worn up
from Los Angeles.

The fortuitous presence of a native at the railroad station
gave them an inkling of where the bus station was to be found,
and they made their way unimpressively through the dark
streets. In the bus terminal's waiting room, while Hanson was
buying the tickets, they tried the vending machines. The
coffee machine gave up after having delivered itself of seven
cups of treacly murk. The Coke machine continued to produce,
and some of the men—the young, rash ones, who cared not
how quickly or violently they came awake—availed themselves
of its products. The men who passed it up placated their gritty
tonsils with bubble gum.

"There's nobody up at this time of night," said Maguire,
"but burglars and bad women."

The bus bumped and ground and twisted its way through the
cold and darkness, past mile after mile of steel-mesh fence.
It turned in at a police gate over which there hung a sign
welcoming the world in general to Fort Burnside, Home of
the Twelfth Infantry Division. Another sign, on a post outside
a long low frame building, made the simple statement: INCOM-
ING TROOPS REPORT HERE. And so they did.

Inside, three or four soldiers milled about behind the counter,
and despite the wretchedness of the hour their faces were alert
and almost friendly.

"Good morning, men," one of them boomed, "and welcome
to Fort Burnside! Find seats close to the front, and a couple of
you come up and pass out these forms."

Gently, almost tentatively, Andy eased himself into a chair
and laid his little flight bag on the floor beside him. Softly, for
a minimum of unseasonal noise. The chair was a schoolroom

chair, one of those ghastly little gadgets with a table top attached, and Andy noticed that every one of them—at least, every one that he could see—had "$11.40" stenciled across its back in white paint.

Carleton, sitting beside him, leaned over and whispered, "Still got the price tag on them. I'm goan buy one for my den." He giggled.

There were perhaps eight blanks on the form to be filled in, stuff such as an unmolested nine-year-old could have written in four minutes, but the sergeant explained every step and every blank as patiently and thoroughly as if they were disassembling an electronic brain. Andy filled out the form without listening, and was far enough ahead of the general trend to catch a few minutes' sleep.

He woke to find himself in a mess hall, drinking coffee and gazing at the top of Maguire's head, which lay on the table across from him. When people started hollering, he awoke Maguire, and the little contingent made its way to something called Initial Clothing Issue.

Andy was not feeling better, but at least he was coming alive. "Uniforms in two sizes," he said. "Too big and too small."

"All right, young soldier," said a corporal on the steps of the building. "We don't talk in ranks around here."

Andy hugged his arms close to his sides and shivered. Lord, this place was cold and clammy! And, come to think of it, there was no assurance that the sun ever came up in this part of the world. Fort Burnside, Land of Eternal Night.

The door opened, letting a little more light slink fearfully out into the cold dark of the street, and a soldier stood in the doorway. "Let's go one time," he said genially. "Let's get these troops out of the hot sun!"

They filed in and took their places against the wall opposite the supply counter, and the normal, comforting confusion of the Army came into its own.

"Sizes thirty-two to thirty-four, over here! Nothing over thirty-four!"

"These long johns you're getting, we call them Superman suits, and you can call them anything you like. You'll probably be hiding them somewhere for the first few days, but then you'll start wearing them just like I do—and you'll be real happy I gave them to you! One thing Fort Burnside gives a man is a healthy, soldierly, hacking cough."

"Fatigue jacket inside the fatigue trousers, and the top button is kept buttoned—unless you're a re-up. An open collar around here means a prior-service man, so don't get casual."

"Now, you won't be getting your Class-A uniform until it's been tailored onto you. But you won't be needing it around here, because you ain't going anywhere anyway."

Andy signed a form labeled "Memorandum Receipt" and sat down on a bench to survey his new wealth of worldly goods. He was now, he found, in possession of 2 drawers, winter; 2 caps, utility; 3 jackets, utility; 3 pr trousers, utility; 2 undershirts, winter; 1 raincoat, dismounted; 1 jacket, shell, field, M-51; 1 overcoat, ctn OG-107, w/removable liner; 1 cap, field cotton; 2 belts, web waist; 1 buckle, web belt, GCM; 1 bag, duffel; 2 towels, bath; 2 neckties, OD-51; 2 insignia, collar, U.S.; 1 copy Field Manual 21-13, *The Soldier's Guide*, and 1 copy Field Manual 21-41, *Personal Conduct for the Soldier*.

He rose and found a full-length mirror and surveyed himself. He had secretly expected that Andy Sheaffer in uniform would be a figure of considerable elegance and dash. He wore clothes extremely well, and the Army uniform is usually one that almost wears itself.

This particular uniform, though, he had never seen before. His first real sight of it, especially with himself inside it, was a withering experience.

In the whole sartorial world, perhaps, there is nothing quite like a brand-new set of Army fatigues. It is not merely that they look awkward and self-conscious and uncomfortable. They seem to have a positive, dynamic, malevolent personality. The material itself is denim, which, as anyone knows who has ever gone through the process of taming a pair of Levis, is hard, stiff, uncompromising stuff. To the basic perversity of this material the Army seems to have added some secret ingredient of its own, some substance that removes all offensive traces of flexibility in the cloth. It does not drape in compliance with gravity; it wanders off in all directions, and there is no flat area in it that does not have knobs and corners and little points to gouge at the skin beneath. Its edges move obligingly aside whenever a cold wind appears in the neighborhood, and welcome in the chilly zephyr. The shirt, carefully tucked in on one side, carefully works its way out to hang sagging on the other side. The trousers, hung or laid flat, will develop bags at the knees. The fly is not happy until it displays incipient gaposis.

And all of it is horribly, gaudily shiny.

Andy looked over the whole ensemble and sadly shook his head. Someday, God wot, they would let him unbutton the collar, and that might help a little. But the cap! Its crown arranged itself in wrinkles and bulges that would never die; its bill curled sinuously off and on his hairline.

He saw a corporal close by, a man whose fatigues looked neat and comfortable and almost respectable. "Pardon me," said Andy. "How do you get your uniform looking that nice?"

"It's easy," said the corporal. "I have the laundry put a little starch in it."

There was something else about the cap, something that seemed somehow out of the way. All the other items of uniform had been painstakingly fitted, and everything was precisely the right size. But not the cap.

Andy went back to the counter and got the attention of the soldier behind it. "The cap," he said. "It seems to be a quarter of a size too small."

The soldier grinned at him. "Just temporary," he said. "You try that cap on an hour from now, and you'll find it fits you perfect."

❖

"In just about three minutes," said Hanson, "they'll start throwing it at us. It makes me tired just thinking about it."

Andy, standing between Hanson's bunk and his own, was already tired without thinking about anything. He rolled his duffel bag over the foot of the bunk, letting it plop unhappily onto the floor, and he put the little flight bag beside it. The mattress was folded in an S shape at the head of the cot; he laid the bedclothes and the pillow on top of it and sat down on the two folded blankets.

Maguire sighed heavily. "Mean-looking hillbilly, that sergeant. He's got a hard mouth."

"Yes," said Carleton, who was sitting on the bare springs of the bunk beyond Hanson's. "I'll bet you it's a big one too."

"Let him surprise me," said Maguire. "I was a flick-major in school, and I didn't go to the movies just to eat the popcorn. He'll just tell us we're not human beings; we're meatheads. We're the lowest form of animal life in this here universe. And we're going to hate the day we ever saw him. That's all he's going to tell us."

"Break it off, Maguire," said Hanson. "He's standing right out there on the porch."

"Are we supposed to be frightened?" said Andy. "There's nothing these people can do to you."

The door opened, and the sergeant came into the squad room. He was a lean, hard, purposeful-looking man in his late thirties, with a glint in his eye and a firmness in his jaw and a faintly belligerent tilt in the Ridgway cap he wore. He came a third of the way down the squad-room aisle, dropped his cigarette into the painted tomato can hanging from one of the wooden pillars, and put both his hands on his hips. "All right, friends," he said, "drop what you're doing and form a little cluster around this here bunk."

"Here we go," Hanson said softly. "Loud and clear."

"You are now in the Second Company of the Service Unit," said the sergeant when they had gathered around him. "My name is Sergeant Schlotzhauer, and the company commander is Captain Showers. You won't be in this company much more than seventy-two hours, and while you here we goan try to make every second count. You'll get up at four o'clock in the morning, and you'll go to bed at nine, and from morning to night you will keep a-humpin'. You with the ducktail haircut over there! You don't smoke until I tell you! Butt it!

"Now. The first deal you gentlemen have to learn in the Army is how to make your bunk. Your mother ain't goan be here to help you out, and I'm goan show you how just once, so you better look alert and listen careful."

His voice was low and matter-of-fact, with none of the expected abusiveness. He laid out the mattress, carefully centered upon it what he called the number-one sheet, and demonstrated the method of tucking in the edges and the corners. "You want your sheets good and tight," he said. "That's what makes your bed. You want to let your sheets work for you."

He made his speech as if he made it every day of his life, and perhaps he did. There was a certain absent-mindedness in his manner, and when he laid the second sheet upon the first, the center of it was not really centered.

"Question, sergeant?" said Carleton.

"Yeah?" said Schlotzhauer.

"How come the sheet hangs lower on this side than it does on the other?"

The sergeant looked blankly at the sheet and then calculatingly at young Carleton. "Because," he said with patient calm, "there's more *of* it on this side."

"Yes, sir," said Carleton. The sergeant adjusted the sheet and continued the demonstration.

"Now, the 'U.S.' on your blanket should come out right about here," he said. He took another look at the blanket. "Well," he said philosophically, "this old blanket don't have no 'U.S.' on it any more. Somebody's done shook the 'U.S.' out a long time ago." He spread the blanket on the bed and tucked it in, and demonstrated how to use the second blanket as a "duster or cap, whichever-so you desire to call it," with its edges coming down no farther than the slat under the spring—and that was it.

"There, now," he said with quiet pride. "There's people will tell you that a bunk when you make it right, you can drop a quarter on it heads and it'll bounce and turn over tails." He studied the young faces about him, and his shoulders gave a small, involuntary shrug. "When you gentlemen can do it that way, then you're goan know you're getting real sharp."

Andy looked at Hanson: When are we going to meet your ogre? Hanson looked back at him: Something's crazy here.

"While you here," said the sergeant, "you goan have a real whirl, a-taking tests, and a-signing papers, and a-listening to speeches, and a-getting your arms shot full of medicine. When you not doing that, you'll be doing chores around the ayrea; we call them dee-tails in the Army.

"This afternoon you'll be going over to the Quartermaster. Tomorrow somebody's goan read you the Articles of War—the Uniform Code of Military Justice is what they call them now. Day after that you'll get your 'flying ten.' That's a ten-dollar bill to take care of you until you're assigned to your unit. You still with me?"

A mumbling affirmative chorus answered him. He looked over the group a little wearily.

"Few minutes from now we goan have a shakedown. I want you to spread out all your personal gear, and we goan come through and tell you what you can keep according to the provisions of Memorandum Twenty. While you're in the Army you won't need your switchblade knives, or any knife over six inches in the blade. If you got one, the blade will be broke and the handle returned to you. If you got brass knuckles or personal firearms we'll save them for you till you get out. And if you got narcotics or hypodermic needles, you are eligible for a personal interview with the company commander.

"There'll be no gambling in these barracks. If you want to make a contribution to the Red Cross, all you have to do is let me walk through the barracks and find a little game going on.

"When you write your next-of-kin to tell them you've arrived and you're in good hands, do not use Second Company as your address, because you not goan be here long enough to get any mail."

He looked at his wristwatch and then at the men again. "Now, if all you young people got sixty cents, you will now meet up with Your Friendly Barber."

One of the men on the outer edge of the circle, emboldened at finding himself still alive and unchewed, spoke to one of his comrades-in-arms. "I haven't got sixty cents," he said, "so I'll pass up the haircut."

The sergeant looked only vaguely in his direction, but in the sergeant's eyes there was a hint of deep inner satisfaction. "They'll jawbone it, young soldier," he said. "You may be poor in this world's goods, but you've always got credit at the barber shop."

❖

In the meeting of two forces so disparate in age and background as American youth and the American Army it would be unreasonable to expect them to agree on every point of taste and necessity. It is a tribute to the innate sensibility of both elements that, with a minimum of discussion, one of them always gives in to the other.

Between the Army and the individual young man, usually the first point of disagreement is reached before the two have even met. It is concerned with whether such a meeting is absolutely necessary to either of them. In most cases the controversy seldom reaches the shouting stage. The youth, with grace and dignity, accedes; and a *mariage de convenance* is negotiated.

The second point of disagreement, met shortly thereafter, is domestic and trivial. The two find themselves worlds apart on the question of how much hair the new soldier needs for beauty, ballast, and protection against the elements.

Contemporary youth is inclined to be extravagant in the matter. It likes a lot of hair, and it likes to fuss over it. In the small contingent of recruits that went up to Fort Burnside with Andy Sheaffer, there were Balboa haircuts, butch haircuts, French butch haircuts, and flat-tops. There were ducktails, reverse ducktails, waterfalls, and whirlwinds. On one head the hair was brushed lovingly up from the temples and elaborately swirled on the top, and the ends of it were strangely tucked into its underbrush. On two of the heads the hair was parted in the back, and on another the eight-inch strands were carefully wrapped around the side and anchored God knows where.

The Army, in its quiet way, seems to feel that hair is all right but that enough of it is enough. In some units it apparently believes that, in the case of the brand-new soldier, enough is somewhat superfluous. Shagginess is excusable on the human chest, and perhaps even admirable there, but the head itself needs no crowning glory except that of a wrinkled prisoner-of-war cap. The hair on the head of a John Recruit should be limited to the brows, the eyelashes, and whatever protudes from the ears and nostrils.

In the Service Unit at Fort Burnside there is only one fashionable coiffure for the new soldier. This haircut, deeply entrenched in the tradition of the outfit, is called the White Sidewall.

It is performed almost ritually. The first man who climbs into the barber chair is asked, with grave courtesy, whether he wishes to keep his sideburns. When he replies that he does, the barber says, "Okay. Hold out your hand."

Up to this point, usually, there has been much hollow laughter and badinage among the nervous waiting customers. Suddenly it all stops as the first little snip is removed. Actually, it is not a snip. It is a swath.

In his right hand the barber holds an instrument that looks like an ordinary electric clipper, except that it is larger. It is also infinitely more thorough. In his left hand, between the fingertips, the barber holds the top of his client's ear. He folds the ear down gently and, almost as if he were picking a spot at random, he dreamily applies the instrument to the skin exposed. It mows a strip, an inch and a half or two inches wide, from the top of the ear to the edge of the crown: a patch of fish-white skin on which not the tiniest stub of hair is left.

Savoring the gasps and painful laughter of the expectant customers lining the wall in front of him, the barber chews off another swath, and another and another, until he has completed the circuit from temple to temple. Then he steps back and looks with pleasant pride upon his handiwork.

It *is* a white sidewall. Dead white. There is hair above it and hair below, but in that ghastly little firebreak itself there is nothing but outraged nakedness.

The men on the bench laugh very loudly, but with no real ring of enjoyment in their laughter. Only the barber, and the cadreman nursemaiding the group, are genuinely amused. The others are in mild shock.

When the barber has rubbed his fingertips across the corridor of ruin, enjoying the polished surface, he cuts a new strip across the very top of the client's head. As like as not, in the ensuing pause some soldier on the bench will moan in aesthetic appreciation. "Man, that is a mystic wig-chop!" or, "The genuine Mohawk, I kid thee not!"

The hair behind the firebreak is the next to go, leaving the front hair as a temporary memorial of what the boy once looked like. This is the next to go. The fringes around the back of his head, ludicrous and obscene, are left until the very last. When they too are gone, nothing remains but livid, lumpy baldness.

The man climbs down, looks at himself ruefully in the mirror, and sits down to rub his ravished scalp in wonder and embarrassment. The latter begins to wane as the next man mounts the chair. Soon all the victims are rubbing one another's heads and laughing. The feeling seems to be that they have been through a hazing and come out sound.

Andy Sheaffer, who had been through many a hazing in his time, was the one recruit who did not laugh at all. Long before his turn came his jaw was set and his eyes were flinty. It was as if, considering his induction an injury, he found the White Sidewall an intolerable added insult.

When his turn came, Sergeant Schlotzhauer lightly clapped him on the shoulder, like a coach sending a man out upon the field. "Let's go," said Schlotzhauer. "Let's get with it."

Andy slowly rose and looked him in the eyes. "Keep your cotton-picking hands off me," he said. "Don't shove."

The sergeant, who had not shoved him at all, looked at him with no excessive concern. "Manners, son," he said to Andy. "Keep your cotton-picking hands off, *please*."

In the astonished hush that followed, Andy made his way to the chair. "Chop away," he said grimly to the barber. "Have yourself a ball."

❖

The rest of the day was, as one of the men expressed it, made in the shade. They had a heavy lunch and a light afternoon, do-

ing trivial chores for some remote divinity called the Labor
Pool, a force that evidently operated on the premise that if
one man can do a given job adequately, a dozen men can
do it twelve times as well. At one point, when fifteen of them
were tidying up the back end of a small recreation hall, Maguire
urged Andy to stop racing his motor. Eventually he did, but
his ignition was still turned on.

After a heavy dinner Schlotzhauer had everybody out in the
company street, where he and a young Negro cadreman named
Clyde marched them up and down and taught them some of
the facing movements.

Clyde was a mellow, dreamy sort. Occasionally, in counting
the cadence, he would say, "Everybody mambo!" and some of
the previous day's recruits would respond, in tempo, "Unh!"
Schlotzhauer was a little sharper, but still restrained. "Git your
interval and cover down!" he would bellow at the formation.
"When I look down this rank I want to see *one head!*" Or,
"Your left foot! The foot on *that* side! And when I say, 'Hut,'
young trooper, that's your hutting foot!" But none of his
language was salty, and his tone was never really harsh.

A couple of times he had halted them and given them a rest
period and told them, "Smoke if you got 'em." The third time
he had merely ordered them at ease, and one of the men assumed that the smoking permission was tacit. The sergeant
gazed toward the smoke. "Son," he said, addressing himself to
whom it might concern, "I hope what I see ain't nothing more
than the steam off'n your breath. Because we don't generally
smoke in ranks around here."

"Well," the recruit said bravely, "I had 'em, so I thought
I'd smoke 'em."

"Well, the way they run the Army these days," said Schlotzhauer, "they often encourage a soldier to think, so I'm not
goan argue with you. If you got 'em, I want you to smoke 'em."

"Sir?" said the recruit.

"You fall out of ranks," said the sergeant, "and set your can down on that retaining wall there, and you smoke 'em till you ain't got 'em any more."

The man sat there, smoking them one after the other, while his fellows marched up and down the street in front of him. He was not forced to smoke the whole pack, though. Schlotzhauer relented when the man had gone through seven.

"I don't know what's got into the Army," Hanson said later, when they were sitting around the barracks, afraid to go out. "It used to be real grim the first few days." He said it as if he were lonesome for the grimness.

At eight, the young Negro cadreman came in and grouped them around him at the foot of one of the bunks.

"My name," he said when they were all settled, "is Clyde— Private Clyde, or Cadreman Clyde, whichever-so you desire. I am *not* a sergeant, but don't you let that make any difference to *you*."

He looked about him in a pleasant, friendly way until he was assured that this part of his orientation had taken effect.

"I am the one in charge of telling you where to go and what to do. There is not a mean bone in my body, and many people go out of this outfit thinking of me almost as a friend. It's no sweat, getting along with Clyde. You do right, and we'll be real tight. On the other hand, if you screw up around here, your behinds will be grass and I will be the lawnmower. Do you read me?"

"Loud and clear," said Maguire.

"The first thing," said Clyde, his voice as mellow as ever, "I want this barracks to stand tall at all times. I want these *floors* to stand tall. These floors are past shining, but I want them clean and pretty. If they not clean, there's people up front going to chew me, and then I'm going to chew you, because that's the way the cooky crumbles. I believe in the Law of the Jungle: an eye for an eye, and everhow else it goes.

"I'm going to show you how to make these beds, and that's how you're going to make them. You're going to make that bed right and tight, and if it isn't, I'm going to come through here and tear it up for you. The government pays me eighty-five dollars and eighty cents a month to tear them beds up, and I'm eager when I do it."

He went through the same bunk-making demonstration that Schlotzhauer had given them that morning, except that his directions were more specific and his corners were tighter, and from time to time he stopped to ask, "Anybody lost?"

No one was lost.

"Now," he said, "as soon as we finish a little GI party I got worked up for you young soldiers—that's a party where I bring the soap and you bring the elbows—you people will then be free and on your own time for the rest of the day. That will amount to about twenty minutes.

"The street over there is as far as you can go thataway, and the PX is your limits in the other direction. Any of you people want to go wandering off somewhere else, don't tense and don't panic and don't be afraid you'll lose your way. The MPs just have to take one look at them civilian shoes and them air-cooled haircuts and they will know who you are and where to bring you back to. Right back here to old Cadreman Clyde. Do you read me?"

"Loud and clear," said the whole assembly.

"Comes nine o'clock," said Clyde, "I want to see every man in his little old bed. You don't want to go to sleep, that's your business. But I will advise you, get your sleep while you can, because we got a busy day planned for you tomorrow. And when that whistle blows in the morning, I want you all to get up *eager*. I want you to look bright-eyed and bushy-tailed and ready for the day. I want everybody to *stand tall*.

"One more thing. Whether you are asleep or not, I want you to *sound* like you're asleep. If I have to come in here after

Lights Out and quiet you people, this whole crew is going to be
out in the street, and I will drill you till you *look* sleepy. Anybody lost?"

"Nobody lost!" said the assembly.

"Good-o," said Cadreman Clyde. "Let's fall to with the
brooms and mops!"

And so they did. It was a strenuous little party, but a not
unpleasant one. At least it gave people something to do.

❖

The cadreman was not a hard man to please. He approved the
results of their labors, stayed around a few minutes to answer
recruits' questions and help them with their buttons and
buckles, and then disappeared.

Precisely at nine o'clock every light in the squad room went
out. They went back on for a minute or two, to allow the men
to find their way to bed, and then the place was dark again.

With the darkness, every noise stopped and every man bur-
rowed a little deeper into his bedclothes. Here and there, from
time to time, there was an isolated sound of sudden exhalation,
or the lonely creak of a bedspring finding its position, but
among the fifty or so men in the room not a single voice was
raised. There was nothing in them that they could have said,
and no one to whom they could have said it. A long way from
home, and in a strange and hostile world, they could only lie
there huddled in the darkness, each one keeping to himself the
ultimate in loneliness, homesickness, misery, and dread.

No one could have given a clearer demonstration of the feeling than a new recruit who at 2045 hours slouched past the
orderly room with his shoulders sloped, his hands in his pockets,
his head upon his chest, and his tail dragging the ground.

Captain Showers, the company commander, was standing on
the low, lighted porch of the orderly room as the recruit passed.
The captain half turned toward where the operations sergeant

sat inside the orderly room. "You did tell them about saluting, didn't you?"

"Yes, sir," said Schlotzhauer. "I sure as hell did."

"Soldier!" Captain Showers roared at the recruit's slowly retreating back. The boy, too numb for trepidity, turned and looked blankly at him.

The captain threw the question that routinely precedes a personal lecture on the hand salute. "How long you been in the Army?"

The boy's look this time was one of unrelieved dejection, and he answered from the bottom of his sad young heart:

"All day, sir."

three

ON HIS FIRST NIGHT in the Army, Andy Sheaffer had had little sleep because he was unaccustomed to sleeping on trains. On his second night, he was too much bothered by his nerves and emotions. On the third night, his left arm was swollen and aching from one of the shots it had received, and he felt as if he had a considerable degree of fever.

On the night after that, nothing could have kept him awake. Dog-tired from lectures, tests, and the simple business of walking around all day, he fell into bed at eight-thirty and was asleep before nine.

All the faces in his dreams that night were indistinguishable, except that some were thin and some were fat, some were in the distance and some wavered cloudily two inches before his eyes. The voices were all a little hollow and remote, and they kept repeating the same few things relentlessly.

"Seventy-two hours to do the job, and every minute counts."

"And notify your family—your mother, father, wife, or dog."

". . . uniform is a proud one. It cost the taxpayers, you and me, one hundred and seventy-two dollars and ninety-one cents."

"Do not lose it. We give you one; you buy the next one."

". . . up at four o'clock and have your chow at five . . ."

". . . under civil law *and* military law. When this lecture is over, you cannot plead ignorance of the latter."

"Catch the sheet approximately one foot from the corner and turn it at a forty-degree angle. This is what we like to call a hospital corner."

". . . not interested in your IQ, but in your *aptitudes!*"

". . . I want to see all them feet going the same way . . ."

"Our shots are given by specialists. They went to school. They can shoot four to five hundred men a day—in both arms."

". . . just grievances, take them to your commanding officer and *he* will take them to the inspector general."

"Improving your swearing will not get you a promotion any faster."

". . . wearing watchchains or fraternity pins on your uniforms, or any other civilian accessories . . ."

". . . have been bathing once a week, and some of you once a month. Here you will use the bathing facilities *daily*."

" . . . any of you Jewish soldiers and Seventh Day Adventists coming in five minutes before the services and expect to be relieved of some detail. You will give your cadremen ample time, ample notice . . ."

". . . collar and *keep* it buttoned."

"You can't have an army without discipline."

". . . room looks like you had *cooks* sleeping in it . . ."

"For the grade of E-1, which is the grade you men are in, that's an income tax of about four dollars a month."

"The latrine is a place where consideration of all is very important."

". . . blade broke off and the handle returned to you."

". . . but eat all you take."

". . . two weeks of furlough and then your second eight weeks in a specialist training outfit . . ."

". . . and assure your folks that the Army medical service and hospitals are second to none."

There was another voice, a wistful feminine voice, very dear but very distant. "You'll never have *your* head in a bag," it said. "You're smooth and slick and quick on your feet, and nothing is ever going to touch you. . . . Andy, I'm not your type."

"That's a gasser," said his own voice. "That's really a gasser." And then his voice, detached from himself, roared with hollow laughter. It was the laughter that woke him at last, a minute or so before the whistle blew at four.

❖

Fatigue was the real commanding officer, and confusion his chief of staff. Footsore and armsore, sleepless and befuddled, Andy found himself abstractly wondering just how long it would be before he dropped from exhaustion, and what the Army could do about it when he did. Then, unexpectedly, it was Sunday morning.

No whistles blew, no voice harassed him, and it was as if the Army itself needed a rest as badly as he did.

He decided at breakfast that he would go back to his barracks and sleep through the rest of the day. The squad room was comparatively quiet, but he found that he himself was restless. He rose and wandered out into the street again.

The morning was warmer and almost sunny. The street was drowsy. Here and there a solitary recruit ambled along with the uniquely pleasant gait of a man who is going nowhere in particular. A little way down the hill a cadreman with a garden hose stood watering the sickly grass, and on the back porch of his own barracks a little group clustered about Private Clyde. Mellow and jocular in civilian sports clothes, Clyde was regaling the recruits and being regaled in turn. Andy turned away; he had no stomach for either.

❖

Madeline Sheaffer came down the stairs and into the living room, shaking her head and sighing. "Arthur," she said, "I wish you'd stop that relentless clumping around down here. You sound like the Shrine circus getting ready to move out."

"I'd like to know," said Arthur, "what else there is to do around here."

"In desperation," she said, "you might even try sleeping. That's what the rest of the world is doing. Do you realize that it's ten-thirty in the morning, and everyone else but you and me is still taking advantage of the fact?"

"I just can't any more. I used to be able to lie abed on Sunday morning without any feeling of sloth. There was something reassuring in listening to the snores from the next room, knowing that they came from a younger and healthier person than myself. This is an eerie household now. I cannot stand the quiet of the place."

"If that's what it is," said Madeline, "go ahead and clump. I must say, though, it doesn't do *me* any good. Clumping is not one of the noises I particularly miss."

Arthur went into the kitchen and returned with two cups of coffee. "I can't stand the neatness of the place, either."

"It's depressingly neat," Madeline conceded.

"I suppose we could toss a dirty old sweatshirt on the piano," said Arthur, "like those blue stars that people used to hang in the window."

"The sight of it," said Madeline, "would set me crying."

"Then don't," said Arthur.

"I wonder if he's neat in the Army."

"I doubt it," said Arthur. "But I suspect that in time he will be. The Army's very fussy about neatness. They'll even teach him how to make his own bed."

"With us," said Madeline, "he never in all his life once had to make his bed. Or straighten his room. Or pick up after himself."

"He will now," said Arthur.

"I can't bear to think of it. He'll come back completely changed. They will have destroyed all of his really most lovable qualities."

"That," said Arthur, "is the one thought that sustains and comforts me."

"Do you suppose," said Madeline, "that if I flew up to where he is these Army people would let me see him?"

"Madeline," said Arthur, "even if they would, at a time like this he probably wants to be left alone."

"I miss him," said Madeline.

"You're supposed to," said Arthur. "That's one of the rules."

❖

Distance muted the shouts from the drill field, where tireless young idiots were playing with a football, and blended them with the faint, discursive organ music that drifted over from the chapel. About the chapel steps some fifteen or twenty soldiers sat waiting unimpatiently for Mass.

Andy wandered back past the mess hall—somewhere inside, Maguire and Carleton were serving their country overtime—and finally came to rest on the low retaining wall in front of the orderly room. The sunshine, such as it was, felt good upon his face.

Across the road, in the visitors' parking strip, little groups of civilians—families, wives, lovers—gathered about their cars, chattering excitedly with their young heroes, whom they had tracked down to this God-forgotten place. Somewhat apart from all the rest an extremely young-looking recruit stood in bittersweet reunion with an extremely young-looking girl. They leaned constantly one toward the other, and his hands played restlessly upon her, awkwardly, hungrily caressing her back and shoulders, her throat and cheek, as they talked. Every few minutes the two of them looked about to see if anyone was watching; then, fleetingly and surreptitiously, kissed.

Andy was suddenly aware that someone was watching them, and that it was he. He closed his eyes and lay back upon the grass. He had once read, somewhere, that every human being on earth feels lonely and alone. He had never believed it, or even understood it, until now.

The people out there, he decided, were from the neighboring towns: Esperanza, La Salada, Smithville, or San Fidel—and none of the soldiers was more than twenty miles from home. That's probably even worse than this. Still, for now, they are together.

Through all the week behind him there had been too little time for thinking and too much time for feeling. His mother, his father, his home had scarcely entered his mind in all those days, and now, in the space of a minute, he missed them more than enough to make up for it. And this was not the worst. There was another thing, something that he had firmly told himself was a matter over and done with. What he would really have liked to see pulling into the parking lot over there was a middle-aged little red Chevrolet convertible and a girl with a pony-tail hairdo.

Footsteps approached, and hesitated briefly, and went on. They stopped at the orderly-room steps, and then there was the sigh of someone sitting down. Andy turned his head and cautiously opened one eye.

It was only Hanson, finding a place to settle.

❖

Sergeant Schlotzhauer came to the orderly-room door to yawn and stretch himself and see what the world was like outside. Finding it quiet and well-behaved, he sat down on the step above the one on which Hanson was sitting.

"Morning," he said. "How they treating you?"

"No sweat," said Hanson. "Cigarette?"

The sergeant inspected the proffered pack and held up his hand. "I can't smoke them beaverboard kind. I got to have the taste of the old-timey, lung-cancer type."

He reached for his own, and the two sat smoking.

"I heard tell," said the sergeant, "they're bringing out a new cigarette. It's got a tobacco-tar tip to screen out the filter. I see old Clyde's down there entertaining the troops. They're a-listening, but their minds is somewheres else."

"I wouldn't be surprised," said Hanson.

"A new recruit in a receiving center," said Schlotzhauer, "you don't even have to look at him to know what he's a-thinking. He's a-thinking wouldn't it be nice if something happened and they'd send him back home. When was you first in?"

"Early 'forty-one. About the first batch they drafted."

"That's when they got me too. And they still ain't turned me loose."

"Let me ask you something," said Hanson. "When are you people going to rear back and put the fear in us?"

"Sometimes," said the sergeant, "they don't *never* get around to it. We ain't supposed to hurt these young people's feelings."

"Used to be," said Hanson, "that's what the Army was for."

"It was nice in the old days," said Schlotzhauer. "I remember how it was when I come in. They'd kick your behind out of

a truck into four foot of snow, and that'd be around four
o'clock in the morning, and they'd give you some coffee, and
maybe some eggs, and then they'd start a-hollering—one guy
a-selling you insurance, and another one a-telling you to send
everything home because you wasn't *never* coming back. And
when they finished talking to you, you knew for damned sure
you was in the Army."

"Around this place," said Hanson, "I haven't even seen one
loud-mouthed Pfc. They used to always have one of those
rank-happy Pfcs around."

"The Lord forgive them," said the sergeant. "They downright
discourage it now."

"No more shock treatment?"

"Not in this outfit."

"Well, how do you get them alert and on their toes? How
do you give them the idea they got a job ahead?"

"If anybody's goan do it," said Schlotzhauer, "it ain't goan
be me. They're a-going to a training outfit; let the training
outfit worry about it. I'll clue you in on one thing, trooper.
I'm tired of getting in trouble over these olive-drab civilians.
I was had up before the IG twice in one month for hurting
draftees' feelings, and I ain't a-going up no third time."

"Hell of a way to run an army," said Hanson.

"I don't know," said Schlotzhauer. "People love to meddle.
It gives the congressman something more to do besides just
mailing out seeds. He can make your boy a Pfc. We may not
be military, but we're sure as hell obliging."

He carefully field-stripped his cigarette, tossed the tobacco
into the street, and tucked the wadded paper into his pocket.
"Let's stop talking shop," he said, "and go git some coffee."

"Hey, Sheaffer!" Hanson called to Andy as they went past.
"You want some coffee?"

"Leave him lay there," said the sergeant. "Coffee would just
wake him up."

Andy lay thinking for four or five minutes; then he opened his eyes and sat up. There was no red Chevrolet in the parking strip across the way, and the young lovers had disappeared.

❖

"Discouraging!" said old Mrs. Daniel, laying her garden tools on a wicker chair and removing her heavy cotton gloves.

"Ma'am?" said Susan, who was sitting at the window, gazing wanly out at the sea.

"Progress, I mean," said her grandmother. "People charging about in all directions. Changing things. Improving things. Eliminating things. Splitting atoms. Curing polio. Sending off rockets to the moon. And nobody ever thinks to do anything about Sunday!"

Susan managed to turn her head toward the old lady and simulate a courteous interest. "What would you like them to do about Sunday?"

"Eliminate it," said Mrs. Daniel. "Root and branch."

"All right," said Susan. "We'll eliminate it."

"How does the water look out there?"

"Cold."

"I think I'll struggle into a bathing suit. Get out there and fight it! Wouldn't do *you* any harm either!"

"I don't feel like a swim," said Susan.

"You don't feel like anything," said her grandmother, "except hanging out the window, watching that dismal ocean."

Having nothing to say, Susan said nothing.

Mrs. Daniel sank into an easy chair and reached for a cigarette. "You're suppose to be looking after me," she said. "Amusing your poor old grandmother. Cheering me up. Watching me. Seeing that I don't break a hip, or whatever it is that old people do. Fine, conscientious job you're doing."

"I guess I'm pretty poor company," said Susan.

"*Wretched* company!" said Mrs. Daniel. "I got quite enthusiastic when you invited yourself up here. Looked forward to a lot of fun and noise. Tiring, but worth it. Look at you, though. Look at me. Which one is the grandmother?"

"I'm sorry," said Susan.

"Why don't you get some men into the place? Why don't you have that Hughes boy over to perk things up? He's an oaf. But, these days, who isn't?"

"He's dull," said Susan.

"Thought that was what you were looking for," said Mrs. Daniel. "That boy in Los Angeles that you're mooning about—you tossed him over because he wasn't dull enough. Call him. Put it on my phone bill."

"I can't," Susan said miserably. "He's in the Army."

"Drafted?"

"No!" said Susan. "He volunteered!"

"I wish you'd told me before," said Mrs. Daniel.

"I don't really want to talk about it," said Susan.

"Like joining the Foreign Legion," said her grandmother. "To forget a woman! An old-fashioned, sentimental, romantic gesture! I envy you!"

"Grandmother," said Susan. "Will you please?"

"Sort of thing your grandfather would have done," said Mrs. Daniel, "if I'd given him the opportunity."

❖

Private Ransom Maguire opened his pocket notebook to the first clean page and began the day's contribution to the journals of his military career.

21. Fatigue uniform as presently constituted is short 1 pocket. Provides 1 pocket each for following items—wallet, handkerchief, cigs, small change etc, notebook and pencil required by Army, & notebook for personal needs. Am

forced to wear field jacket whether need or not, to have place for pocket radio.

22. In this whole clutch of draftees, only me, Hanson, and Sheaffer old enough to be served at a saloon. What ever happened to old fashioned child labor laws. Grand little group, this. Hanson dull, Sheaffer sulky, Carleton eager and too Dam cheerful. The 2 Mexicans still huddled together, possibly for warmth, but rumor says they are joined together at the hip.

23. 1st Sgt talking yesty to company clerk mentioned some joker getting discharged on a 368. Question: what is a 368 & how do you work it. Check this.

24. Dependent can initiate dependency allotment herself if you dont. Class Q Allotment to the late Mrs. Maguire will be $117.10 a mo., $30.00 of which comes from undersigned's pay envelope. May she choke on it.

25. By setting wristwatch forward 4 or 5 hrs. a man cd emotionally adjust to Army schedule. Would rise early (8 or 9 a.m.) but rest of days activities wd be carried out at a decent and civilized time of day. O Maguire, you are a dreamer.

26. Sell the small car & buy Federated Petroleum preferred. Down 3⅛ since Thursday.

27. 1st KP into the mess hall in the morning gets 1st choice of jobs. Last man in gets grease trap. Question: what is grease trap. Check.

❖

At seven-thirty the next evening they were turning their bedding in, and lading themselves with duffel bags and A-wol bags,

and pounding the shoulder of Cadreman Clyde. At eight o'clock
they were milling about a loading shed, waiting for the buses
that were to take them to a training company somewhere on
the same post.

Among the hundred or more of them, Andy spotted perhaps
a dozen of his comrades from the original Los Angeles contingent. Maguire was there, and Hanson, and young Carleton, and
the two Mexicans, both looking as lost and unhappy and un-
communicative as ever.

Then a hoarse private first class was herding them aboard
the first of the buses. Except for his voice, he was a spectacularly
ordinary type. Hanson, pulling himself into the bus behind
Andy, chuckled happily.

"What's the matter?" said Andy, trying to look back around
the bulk of his duffel bag.

"First sign of home I've seen all week," Hanson whispered.
"The loud-mouthed Pfc."

In the front seat, lounging like one of the latter Caesars,
sat a small, dark, sturdy-looking young man with the four
stripes of a sergeant. The stripes were repeated on the front
of his headdress, which was a plastic helmet liner painted
baby-blue and polished to a blinding degree. His other ac-
couterments included a web belt three inches wide, with a corre-
spondingly large brass buckle plate, a swagger stick with a
pair of yellow gloves wrapped around it and held in place by
a rubber band, a pair of ornate brass insignia pinned to the
shoulder straps of his shirt, seven service ribbons (two of them
in gilt frames), a combat-infantryman's badge, and a name plate
over his right shirt pocket. The name plate said: STORMCLOUD.

"You tell me," he said, "if I'm in anybody's way." His
eyes were half-closed, and his whole expression was a bland
mixture of affability and sheer laziness. Passing him, Andy
looked closer at him and decided that neither of these admirable traits was real. The eyes were much too keen.

"Can you guys shine shoes?" said the sergeant. "Make up beds? Crawl in cadence?"

"Goodness, no!" replied one brave young trooper in the rear of the bus. "We just pick up the phone and call room service."

"That's the kind of men we need," said the sergeant. "We're going to get along real good."

"Where we going, sergeant?" someone else shouted.

Sergeant Stormcloud smiled dreamily. "You're going to an outfit just made for you. Fox Company of the Seventy-First Infantry. The sloppiest, easiest old rout-step outfit in the Army. Just settle back and take it easy from now on. Nobody gives a damn for nothing in Fox Company."

four

HALF A MILE across the post the permanent-party personnel of Fox Company forgathered in the two little adjoining offices at the end of the orderly room. Those who could find space were settled in the inner office, the throne room of the company commander. The others milled about the anteroom, which was the first sergeant's, or wandered in and out through the door connecting the two.

The gathering was informal. The company commander, First Lieutenant Jesse L. Jennison, sat behind his desk, sighting along his swagger stick at the supply sergeant, who leaned against the wall beside the door. Second Lieutenant Oscar M. Taylor sat behind the other desk, morosely studying a game of Idiot's Delight. The third officer, Second Lieutenant Murray J. Tighler, sat in the space chair with his legs extended straight out in front of him.

The first sergeant sat at his own desk outside, paying no attention to anything except the orders he was reading.

"Shehan," the company commander was saying to the supply sergeant, "I don't give a damn where you were going or what you were planning to do. So just don't give me no hard time." His voice was laboriously jocular.

"Lieutenant," said the supply sergeant, "if you want to put it on that basis, all right. If that's the kind of company you want to run. I'll just send the girl a flushogram and sacrifice my whole evening."

"Total war," said Lieutenant Tighler.

"We're forming this company tonight," said Lieutenant Jennison, "and we're going to form it up proper. I want every man in this cattery to show me a conspishously outstanding performance."

"Shehan is the one I love to hear talk to them," said Lieutenant Taylor. "He's had advantages we haven't. He went to military school."

Sergeant Fenwick, the only four-stripe man in the room, smoothed the fold of the gloves wrapped around his swagger stick. "I wish I'd gone to military school," he said.

The first sergeant came to the office door, pushing the company clerk gently out of the way. "I wish you draftees would break it up," he said, and it was evident that the classification included everyone there except himself. At thirty-five, First Sergeant Hanna was the oldest man in the group. He was also unquestionably the most professional military man on the premises, and his attitude of avuncular tolerance extended even to the officers of his company.

"It's not a *bad* roster," he said, taking off his glasses. "It's a sight more promising than that bunch of lardheads they sent us yesterday."

"Any rank in it?" Lieutenant Jennison asked.

Hanna slid the paper across the company commander's desk. "Couple of E-fives. One corporal. Handful of prior-service men in the rear ranks."

Sergeant Fenwick spoke up. "I just want to know one thing, Lieutenant. What's the policy going to be this cycle? We going to treat these children like their mothers did, or we going to treat them like they were in the Army?"

Jennison looked at him with a faint smile. "You got a closer choice than that, Sergeant Fenwick, and I don't have to familiaritize you with it. You want to satisfy the mothers, or you want to satisfy the regimental commander?"

"You got two things to remember," said the first sergeant, "and that goes for all of you. First, let them know they've got a job cut out for them. Second, don't let up on them. Keep them busy and keep them guessing. Stay one step ahead of them all the way."

"And third," said Lieutenant Tighler, "don't borrow money from them."

"Hold it," said Lieutenant Taylor, cupping his ear. "That's the buses. Here come the bodies!"

❖

The relaxed joviality of the bus ride came to an abrupt halt at the head of the company street. The bus had hardly stopped when Stormcloud and the private first-class leaped out of it. The street filled immediately with noise and confusion, and it seemed as if the whole world were shouting at the recruits, nagging at them, snapping at their heels.

"Come on come on come on, let's go!" roared a voice heavy with dislike. "*Move!*"

"Pick it up! Pick it up!" shouted another. "You people move like a bunch of washwomen!"

"Come on, young hero!" snarled a third. "You're not in a Cub Scout patrol!"

"What have you got down there?" said a mighty voice from the orderly-room porch. "A herd of sick buffaloes? Fall them men into four ranks!"

"Your position is *attention!*" said the Pfc. "Get them heads back and look right through me!"

"Sloppy," said the lieutenant on the porch. "Very sloppy. Put some wrinkles in their chins, sergeant!"

"Let's get them heads *up!* When I look at you people I want to see a wrinkle in every chin! I want to see *statues!* Heads back and your chins in!"

"Suck that gut in, soldier!" the Pfc snapped at Andy. Andy rearranged himself as stiffly as he could.

"You don't look at me when I speak to you!" the Pfc screeched. "You look *through* me! Oh, I tell you, you people got a long ways to go!"

At least a dozen voices were screaming at them simultaneously —the lieutenants on the porch, the first sergeant down below, the cadremen prowling restlessly and irritably up and down and in and out of the ranks.

"You're *sorry?*" Andy could hear someone saying somewhere down the line. "Now isn't that just *dandy!*"

"You people got short memories or something?" the first sergeant shouted. "You daydreaming? I want them chins tucked in! I *want* them exaggerated!"

"You, hero," said the Pfc, "you don't have that chin in!"

"Those caps are two fingers above the bridge of the nose! And unbutton those silly-looking collars; you're not recruits any more. Pull that collar higher, soldier! I want to see that clean white T-shirt!"

The querulous voice of one of the lieutenants zoomed down from the orderly-room porch. "What are those people moving their *hands* around for?"

"Pull that hat down!" said a voice behind Andy. "Put that tag in your pocket! Get that head and eyes straight to the front!"

"What's your name?" said someone off to the left somewhere. "You don't look at me, young man; I look at you!"

"Group," said the first sergeant, "attench-hun! Parade! rest! Oh, look at that!" He looked at it himself with a look of immeasurable despair and weariness. "All right, let's do it again! Group! Attench-hun! Parade! rest!"

"You people never heard of parade rest?" roared the five-striped sergeant beside him. "At the command, 'rest!' you people will move your left foot smartly twelve inches to the left of your right foot, and I want to hear those feet *hit!* At the same time, with your arms hanging naturally behind your back and below the belt line, you will clasp your right hand loosely with your left hand, the fingers of your right hand extended and joined and both palms extended to the rear, head and eyes as at the position of attention! You will keep your mouth shut and you will not move!"

"Group," said the first sergeant, "attench-hun! Parade! rest!"

"Sloppy!" said the other lieutenant on the porch.

"Your hands in the small of your back!" said the Pfc.

"Straighten up those sloping backs!" yelled another cadreman in the dim distance.

"You don't shake your head when I ask you something, young fellow!" said another voice. "You say, 'No, *sir'!*"

"No, *sir!*"

"Go down to that fourth-platoon barracks," the senior lieutenant said to one of the noncoms, "and bring out that other detachment of the walking dead."

A voice down toward the end of the formation was fraught with exasperation. "I'll do the thinking; you be the *robot!* You can think for yourselves later, but *not now!*"

"Group," said the first sergeant, "attench-hun!"

"Slap those feet all at the same time!" somebody shouted.

A corporal with a clip board stood before the formation. "I'm going to call you people's names," he said, "and when I call yours, I want you to sound off! 'Here, *sir!*' Nothing here but 'Here, *sir!*' And if I hear one weak voice, that man is going to wish he never lived!"

That wouldn't be difficult, Andy said to himself.

"Those men are supposed to be at *attention!*" said one of the lieutenants.

"All right!" said the corporal. "You people come to attention! When I say attention, I want to see a ramrod down your back and sixteen wrinkles in every chin!"

"Pull those fat civilian bellies in!" said the first sergeant.

"Tell those people to suck some air into those puny civilian chests," said the lieutenant.

His voice was drowned out by a wave of humanity charging up the company street at a half-run, shouting as it came. Whatever the wave was, it was called to a halt and brought to attention. As the corporal addressing Andy's contingent began calling the names on his roster, the five-stripe sergeant began harassing the troops in the other contingent.

"You people been in this company all day, and you haven't shown anybody a *thing!* You seem to think that when it gets dark around here, you're supposed to sack in and start *snoring!* Well, you're not! You're on twenty-four-hour shift in this company! You move on the double at all times! And you sound off as you move! And you do not sit down or lie down unless you are safely certain that you're just about to *die!*"

The sergeant was still haranguing them when the corporal finished calling the new men's roster. "Group!" said the corporal, and there was an immediate rustle among the men in the formation. "All right!" said the corporal, his face contorted with exasperation. "Some of you people are anticipating my command! It displeases me highly when someone anticipates my command! You will hang upon my every word, but you will *not* anticipate me! Group!"—utter stillness—" 'Tench-hut!"

"There's still some people *late* around here!" said the Pfc. "There's still some people *daydreaming!*"

At a command from the first sergeant, the five-striper moved his own contingent to touch upon the other, and the senior lieutenant on the porch rapped on the railing with his swagger stick.

❖

"Men," said the lieutenant, "my name is Lieutenant Jennison. I am commanding officer of Company F, Seventy-First United States Infantry Regiment. You men are fortunate enough to have been assigned to this company. Fox Company has the best cattery, the best officers, and the best reputation on this post or parts adjutant thereto. While you are here you will be a representative member of this company, and you will uphold that tradition at all times.

"You men have prollably been told that the first impression is the important one. I want to tell you that the first impression you have made on me is the sorriest I have ever seen. You got off those buses like molasses on a cold day, and you stand around now like you all had the rickets.

"The first thing you people want to do is to get it into your thick heads that you are no longer a bunch of college boys, bellhops, civilians. You can forget what you used to do in the past, and what you plan to do in the future, because at this moment you've got no past and you've got no future.

"You people are the lowest thing in the United States Army. Remember that. You have got eight long, ardious, strainious weeks ahead of you, and you are going to live life to the fullest during all that time. You are not here to be harassed or petted. You are here to be trained. Our job is to mold you people into first-class fighting machines, and we intend to do that with or without your cooperation. Does everybody understand that?"

"Yes, sir!" the assembly responded with somewhat less than fanatic zeal and volume.

"I don't hear you," said the lieutenant. "When I ask you a question I want to hear the answer loud and enthusiastic. I want to hear those little throats throb till hell won't have it. Does everybody understand that?"

The answer this time could have been heard halfway to La Salada. "Yes, *sir!*"

"By the time your eight weeks are up, you people are going to be the best-looking, best-trained company on this post. This will represent a one-hundred-per-cent improvement, because you are now the worst-looking bunch of eight-balls I have ever looked upon! You are the personication of conspishous medioc-racy! First sergeant, take over!"

Merciful God, said Andy, how long can they keep this up? Have I been pulled into this fantastic world to be talked to death?

❖

All three of the lieutenants wheeled and disappeared into the orderly room, and Sergeant Hanna faced the group. In contrast to the company commander's rolling and fanciful delivery, the first sergeant's was clipped and icy, but the content of his remarks was the same.

"My name," he said, "is First Sergeant Kenneth V. Hanna, and you people are going to see a lot of me! The less you see of me, the happier you're going to be!"

"Your feet are *together*, soldier!" someone said to Andy. He brought his feet together—quickly.

"My office is known as the orderly room," the first sergeant continued, "and when you come in there, you come in through channels! You get your squad leader's permission to ask your platoon sergeant for permission to see me! You knock before you enter, and you take off your little cap! And unless you come reporting for work, or punishment, or some other good military reason, God help you! Is that clear?"

"Yes, *sir!*"

"When you are called for a formation, no matter where you are in the company area, you have exactly thirty seconds to make that formation! In this company area you will double-time everywhere you go! And outside this company area you will not go at all unless you are taken! Is that clear?"

"Yes, sir!"

"I said, is that clear?"

"Yes, *sir!*"

"When you hear your name coming over the bitch-box, you will drop everything and come running! You will fall out of your cozy bunks tomorrow morning at five-thirty—and that does not mean five-thirty-two or five-thirty-one!

"You will keep yourselves and your quarters and your equipment looking shipshape and Bristol-fashion at all times! Every shoe will be shined to a sparkle, and any time I look at a shoe I want to see my own reflection in it! When I inspect your barracks, I will look them over from stem to gudgeon, and I don't want to see them looking like a damned hogpen! Some of you men that came in last night have been a little remiss! I have found cigarette butts in the area! If I continue to find cigarette butts in the area, you men can count on giving up smoking altogether! Is that clear?"

"Yes, *sir!*"

"Everything has a purpose. My purpose is to make trained, efficient soldiers out of you. You men can make it easy on yourselves or hard on yourselves, and I don't particularly care which, because I can play it both ways. Goof up once—just once—and you men have had it! You can lay your hearts upon the altar, for your tails are mine! Are there any questions?"

"No, *sir!*"

"That's all I have to say, then, except one thing. The last thing on earth you people want to do is irritate *me!* You want to make me *happy!* That's your main purpose in life! Understood?"

"Yes, *sir!*"

He gave the formation a slow study that seemed to take in individually every face in every rank and find each face more displeasing than the last.

"All right. then," he said. "Platoon sergeants, take over!"

❖

The command was Left Face, and with it the hope rose in Andy Sheaffer's gullet. Now he was turned in the direction of home. One of the barracks buildings ahead had a bunk reserved for him. It might not be a warm bunk, it almost certainly would not be pliant, but at least it would be stationary—and this was what Andrew J. Sheaffer wanted, at the moment, more than anything else in life.

In less than twenty seconds it developed that they were not going to their barracks. More than that, it seemed that the Army of the United States could not make up its mind where they were going.

"About! face!" came the command, and two hundred young bodies spun awkwardly about on the tips of their right toes. Two hundred numb young faces looked toward the head of the company street.

"About! face!" The command was repeated, and they faced the foot of the street. It came a third time—"About! face!"—and none of them knew or cared any longer in which direction they were aimed.

"F'wurd! harch!" And away they went.

The voice that kept shouting at them now was that of Sergeant Stormcloud. The little Indian's face was no longer placid; his eyes were no longer lazy. He was awake, and alert, and appallingly energetic. Standing in the center of the company street, rhythmically slapping his trouser leg with his swagger stick, he seemed to be playing a game that only he could enjoy. He was demonstrating how many sides they could pass him on without his having to move from the spot.

"By the left flank, harch! By the left flank, harch! To the rear, harch! By the right flank, harch! By the left flank, harch!" And then, over and over and over again, "To the rear, harch! To the rear, harch!"—until the whole company was a mass of hopelessly mingled lone wolves going in all directions at once: sidestepping, bumping into one another, fervently wishing that a bolt of lightning would come down and burn this savage little sergeant to a crisp.

When everything was a mishmash he had them all formed up again, and then he continued as before. Up and down and sidewise they marched, having no idea of what they were doing or how, conscious of nothing but the narrowness of that little street and the relentlessness of Stormcloud's voice bouncing off the barracks on both sides of them—or sometimes before or behind them. One command had hardly begun echoing when the next rolled in and smothered it. All sense of time was lost, and then all sense of reality.

The two rows of barracks between which they milled were soon the only lighted barracks in the whole area. While they marched up and down, the rest of the Army was going to sleep.

At last it was over, or so it seemed, and they were filing through a supply room, drawing their bedding. With bedding and duffel bags and personal gear and everything else, they were at last in the warmth and security of their own quarters.

Andy fell upon a bunk, and flopped against the S-shaped roll of mattress at one end, and closed his eyes for a minute. A little refreshed, but not much, he looked about the squad room for a friendly face. Maguire was nowhere in sight, nor was the grinny little Carleton, but down toward the latrine end of the room one of the Mexican kids sat desolately alone. Someone sat down heavily on the bunk behind Andy, and it was the prior-service man, George Hanson.

"I'm going to die," said Hanson. "I'm going to die."

"This is the way you wanted it," said Andy. "This is the Army you were so damned homesick for. I hope you're happy with it."

"I've seen some gung-ho outfits in my day," said Hanson, "but this one is the worst. I stood out there and listened to those people, and my lower lip was hanging down to here."

The door at the far end of the squad room burst open and a cadreman charged into the place. "What are you people sitting around for?" he screamed. "Let's be getting those bunks made! You want to sleep on the floor or something? Let's go one time!"

Hanson moved away, and Andy began putting the cover on his mattress. He was working on the number-one sheet when a mechanical voice came through the intercom. "Third P'toon." A second later this was repeated. After a pause, the voice became a snarl. "All right, you Third P'toon meatheads. You want to answer that bitch-box, or you want me to walk down and answer it for you?"

Someone found the switch on the intercom box and cautiously answered, "Third Platoon."

"Third P'toon, *sir*," said the instrument.

"Third Platoon, *sir*," said the frightened recruit.

"Private George W. Hanson," said the box. "Tell him to get his behind to the orderly room. On the double."

"Oh, Lord," said Hanson, and then he was gone.

Andy was tucking the second blanket in when the box sounded off again. All platoons were to fall out in the company street for more dismounted drill.

❖

Much, much later they dragged themselves back up the barracks steps and into the squad room. "What time is it?" someone asked Andy.

"I don't know," said Andy, "and I don't want to look. You're just torturing yourself, that way."

One of the men fell heavily upon his bunk. "Wake the town and tell the people," he said. "I am dorked. Bugged. Bushed. Beat."

"These shoes," said Andy, sitting on the edge of his own bunk. "They weigh more than I do, and they're a good deal tougher." He was reaching down to untie a shoelace when the door opened at the far end of the room and the small Indian sergeant came bouncing in.

"Everybody feel good?" he boomed. "Everybody bright-eyed and bushy-tailed? Everybody anxious to excel?"

"Sergeant," said a small, weary voice, "do like the wind does. Please?"

Stormcloud clapped the man heartily on the shoulder. "Son," he said, "we're just getting started!"

There was a strange thing about Stormcloud. As crisp and rugged as he was as a drillmaster, the second that he had given the men Fall Out he was as mellow and friendly as anyone could possibly be. There must be a reason, Andy reflected. This cadreman must be unusually sure of himself.

"Sergeant," he called as Stormcloud passed his bunk, "may I ask a question?"

"That's what I'm here for," said the sergeant. "That's the only way you're ever going to learn anything."

"What's your job around here?"

"Not much of anything," said Stormcloud. "I'm just what they call the Field First Sergeant."

"What does that mean?"

"It means when we get out of earshot of the orderly room I'm practically the commanding general. The lieutenants drink coffee. The first sergeant does paper work. I do the hollering and make you people into soldiers."

"We're awful grateful for things like that," said Andy.

Stormcloud turned abruptly and addressed the room at large. "All right, fellows," he said. "There's still a little time before we start getting sleepy. Might as well put it to use. Let's get these barracks straightened up.

"It's five minutes after twelve now. Army don't like to have to pay overtime, so let's play a little trick on the Army. Let's some of you men get over and tack blankets over the windows.

"Two of you run up to the supply room and get some soap and brushes.

"Now, all this asphalt tile on this floor looks real gray and scuffy-looking to me. What we want to do is buff it up good and make that tile real nice and shiny. Then, if we tie a thread around the center of the squad room, and walk on the outside of that thread, we can keep it looking good. Okay?"

Okay, said Andy to himself. Let's just do it. Let's not strive for Group Spirit.

"What are we going to use for a buffer?" someone asked.

"We should have got the buffer out of the orderly room before somebody else did," said Stormcloud. "Now we're going to have to do it the old-fashioned way. Between the bunks, and under the bunks, and behind the bunks, just take the wool socks you were issued. They'll make very good buffers. And for the center of the room—"

He looked about until his eyes lit on an especially large young man. The trainee, Andy noted, was the fat boy from his own Los Angeles contingent, the kid who had constantly scratched his backside in the meat line.

"What do you weigh, trooper?" the sergeant asked him.

The young man flushed. "Two hunnert and fifteen," he said.

Stormcloud whipped a blanket off the nearest bunk and spread it on the floor. "Sit in the middle of that," he said.

"Now, if two of you men grab the front corners of that blanket, and one of you grabs the back, and give that boy a ride, we're going to have the best little old buffer there is. If you want to give something a real polish, you got to do it by hand."

The place was full of bustle and noise for more than an hour before the sergeant gave the word—"Break it off." They broke it off with touching gratitude and relief.

"I see it is now oh-one-thirty-five hours," said Stormcloud. "We've got lots to do tomorrow, so I want you young people to get a good night's sleep. Let's flake out on our little pads and make the most of it."

At two o'clock the lights went off.

At four o'clock they came on again, and whistles blew, and loud voices importuned them to rise and greet the day.

Damn it, said Andy, this is just too much.

Splashing water upon his face, he turned to the man at the next sink and gave voice to his burning sense of outrage. "That first sergeant practically *promised* us," he said, "that we could sleep till five-thirty."

five

ARTHUR SHEAFFER had just begun looking through his morning mail when his secretary stuck her head in at the door. "There's a Miss Daniels or Daniel on the phone," she said. "She says it's personal."

"Of course it's personal," said Mr. Sheaffer. He carefully

straightened his necktie and then picked up the phone. "Good morning, my dear!"

"Good morning," said Susan.

"Where the devil have you been?"

"Visiting my grandmother. I'm just in town to do a few errands, and I got thinking of you."

"That's very flattering," said Arthur.

"Mr. Sheaffer," said Susan, "are you having lunch with anyone today?"

"As a matter of fact," said Arthur, without even looking at his calendar, "I'm not."

"May I buy lunch for you?"

"No," said Arthur, "but if you feel philanthropic I'll let you leave the tip."

❖

There was a fearful lot of hustle and bustle in Fox Company that morning—a magnificent display of neat military confusion. Someone in the orderly room must have sat up half the night, planning it down to the last precise detail of chaos.

It was Moving Day.

During the night the company commander, or the first sergeant, or whoever it was, had re-formed the whole company on paper. Using some master plan beyond the ken of ordinary mortals, he had transformed five bloblike barrackfuls of bodies into five infantry platoons and set the stage for a game of military musical chairs.

While the breakfast pots and pans were still being banged about in the mess-hall kitchen, the noncommissioned personnel of Fox Company were delightedly shoving and shouting and moving the men from building to building, settling them down in their new places. It was no easy task; the bodies they were shifting were numb with weariness and lack of sleep, and quite happy with the barracks they had—if, of course, barracks were inevitable.

Maneuvering his mountain of gear into the barracks to which he had been assigned, Andy heard himself being paged. "Mr. Sheaffer! Mr. Sheaffer! This way, please! The presidential suite awaits you!"

He looked in the direction of the voice, and there was Maguire, perched cross-legged on a mattress of a corner bunk. The bunk next to it was empty, and on the third bunk Carleton was grinning at him.

"I thought you'd like to be with us," said Maguire, "and the view from here is really quite exquisite!"

"Hi there, young soldier," said Carleton.

"Well!" said Andy, plopping his gear on the center bunk. "Who arranged all this?"

"Your old daddy," said Maguire. "Who else? While you troops were shlepping around last night I was down in the orderly room, providing for the improvident."

"What's he talking about?" Andy asked Carleton.

"He's just sliding his jib again," said Carleton. "I can't get tuned in on him."

"I understand they gave you troops a rough time last night," said Maguire. "Like the company commander would say, 'ardious and strainious.' I sat there and brooded about you boys. My heart bled for you."

"Sat where?" said Andy. "Bled where?"

"Down in the orderly room," said Maguire, "there with the rest of the country-club element, listening to the far-off sounds of battle. I said to myself, Those are *my* men out there bleeding."

"You're leaving out some of the exposition," said Andy.

"So I am," said Maguire. "The way it all happened, I was sent on an important mission to pick up the floor buffer, and somebody else had beat me to it, and I saw that the company clerk was having trouble with his paper work, and you know how obliging I am about volunteering."

"Everybody knows that," said Andy.

"I lent a hand to the company clerk, meanwhile eavesdropping on the conversations in the first sergeant's office. Then I went over and helped out the supply sergeant—very nice guy; one of nature's noblemen—and as a result I am a military expert."

"That's what we've been needing around here," said Andy.

"The company commander is not only a hillbilly but a draftee as well. He's what they used to call a ninety-day wonder. The first sergeant is supposed to be the sharpest one in the regiment. Stormcloud is an eager beaver, a full-blooded Comanche Indian, a guy who wants to spend the rest of his life in the Army. That big-mouthed Pfc, Polier, is only the mail clerk around here. And the poop is that Fox Company actually *is* the best outfit in the regiment."

"All right, Louella," said Andy, secretly quite impressed, "what's your next exclusive?"

"My next exclusive," said Maguire, "is who's going to be platoon sergeant of this platoon."

"What's a platoon sergeant?" Carleton asked.

"That's just the sergeant who has the power of life and death over everybody in this barracks. He runs the whole sh-boom."

"So?" said Andy. "Who? Victor McLaglen?"

"Hanson," said Maguire. "Hanna's going to make him a Hollywood sergeant."

Andy laughed. "Maguire, you're out of your skull."

Carleton made a quick horizontal motion with his hand. "Chop it," he said. "Here comes the government."

The booming Pfc Polier had just come in through the door at the far end of the room.

"I'll tell you the rest this afternoon," Maguire whispered. "We've all been invited to the labor pool."

Pfc Polier stood just inside the door and glared ferociously at the assembly. "Well!" he bellowed. "You people got a lot to learn around here! I suppose nobody's told you people the policy of this company when a cadreman walks into the barracks!"

"No, sir," said the man nearest him.

"All right, then!" said Polier. "I will tell you! The policy of this company, when a cadreman walks into the barracks, somebody hollers attention and the rest of you brace! You got that?"

"Yes, sir," said the entire group.

"All right, we're going to try it again! And the nearest man to the door *sounds off!*"

He stepped out, closing the door behind him, waited a few seconds, and stepped in again.

"Attention!" came the tremulous tenor cry.

"At ease, men," said Polier. He walked to the center of the room, the portion that should by rights have been roped off with thread, and gazed majestically about him. His eyes came to rest upon Andy.

"What's so funny to you, trooper?" he shouted.

"Not a thing," said Andy, omitting the "sir." He felt no inclination to kowtow to a mail clerk.

"All right, then," said Polier. "Wipe that smile off your face."

Andy lifted a hand to his mouth, slowly wiped the smile off, and looked mockingly at the cadreman. The latter looked back at him without amusement.

"Trooper," said Polier, "you show promise of being a trouble-maker, and I thrive on that type. It's my policy to always give a dog or a damned fool one chance. Consider you've just had yours."

He glared at Andy for several icy seconds, then cleared his throat and looked about him. "All right, you people," he said, butting his cigarette on a tomato can hanging from a post, "gather around and give me your undivided. The first thing we're going to learn is how to make a bed."

❖

Arthur Sheaffer seated her gravely at the table, wedged himself into his own seat, and gave her his warm and wonderful smile. At my time of life, he reflected, a man should be subjected once a day to a sight as young and pretty and nice as this.

Her costume was, in the older and calmer sense of the word, quite revealing. It was a gray shirtwaist dress, with white collar and cuffs, and a little black bow at the throat. It takes a good deal of imagination and dash, he decided, to look so unconvincingly prim and conservative.

He noted, and filed it away in his mind, that she had no packages with her. She probably had no errands, either.

"How's everybody?" she asked when she had finished smiling back at him.

"Madeline's fine," he said. "Just fine."

"And Andy?"

He chuckled. "Is that an afterthought?"

"No, sir."

"He's probably in spectacular shape, although I'm just guessing when I say it. We had a little note from him at the place where he's being processed. He says they're keeping him horribly busy, and I don't think he's quite adjusted to being kept busy."

"I feel terribly, Mr. Sheaffer," she said. "I mean, about what happened."

"Going into the Army?" said Arthur. "Nonsense, my dear. I'm quite exhilarated by it. It's rather like sending him off to nursery school."

"Mrs. Sheaffer says it's my fault," said Susan. "And she's right."

Arthur looked at his whisky sour to avoid Susan's eyes. He had not been aware that the child had even talked to Madeline. "Is it?" he said.

"If we hadn't fought," said Susan, "he wouldn't have been upset, and he'd have passed his exams as easily as always, and he wouldn't be in the Army at all. He must resent me terribly."

"I have heard," said Arthur, "that young people fight all the time, but comparatively few of them end up in the Army because of it. I can't see that one thing has anything to do with the other." She shook her head in unhappy contradiction.

"Was it at least a good fight?" said Arthur. "Zestful? Enjoyable?"

"It was a nasty fight," said Susan, "and I wish it hadn't happened. Oh, I must have been feeling awfully righteous that day! I told him he was shallow and idle and a wastrel—"

"Good heavens!" Arthur laughed in deprecation. "That's nothing unusual. I've been telling him that all his life."

"Is he all those things?" said Susan. "Really?"

Arthur looked at the earnest little V between her eyebrows and felt a bittersweet little pang of empathy and compassion. "I don't know, my dear," he said slowly. "I've always rather suspected that he isn't. We'll both find out eventually."

"I don't think he'll write to me," said Susan. "I think I told him not to, and he doesn't even know my address."

"And now," said Arthur, with a commiserative little smile, "you think you told him prematurely?"

"All I know," said Susan, "is that I miss him very much."

"Then that makes two of you moping," said Arthur. "It looks as if the next move is yours."

❖

Extracts from the notebooks of Ransom Maguire, Private E-1, Army of the United States (temporary):

56. Barracks guard has good position. Vy important function with abs. nothing to do. Day room orderlies & game room orderlies excused from K.P., police & barracks detail. Drivers have good deal. Sleep in the vehicles.

57. H. Carleton wants to borrow pencil to figure out months wages. Asked him whats the matter, havent you got fingers. Carleton gets letters from a girl with S.W.S.S. T.H.T.D.T.T. on the back of envelope. Carleton says means sealed with sufficient saliva to hold the Dam thing together. How quaintsey can one get.

58. Ft Burnside now plastered with orders to conserve legal size paper. At least 1 copy of memo on evy bulletin board on post. Memo printed on legal size paper. Another memo now is Reporting Unidentified Submarines. Says if submarine is sighted from an aircraft, that should be mentioned in the report. Roger. Wilco. Over and out.

59. For bivouack. What wd be extra weight involved in taking 2 boxes candy bars on bivouack for resale out there in the boondock. Candy cost at P. X. is prob 4 cents a bar, cd be resold 2 for 25.

❖

Seen at close range, especially by one of his enlisted men, First Lieutenant Jesse L. Jennison was a terrifying tribute to the manufacturing skill of Officer Candidate Schools. In his recent boyhood, somewhere deep in the rural South, it is quite probable that he had a slouching walk and a soft and casual manner. His only casualness now was in his approach to the English language, to which he gave much more than he took.

Lieutenant Jennison was now, to all appearances, a finely

constructed military machine with clean straight lines and a powerful overdrive. The straightness of the lines was most pronounced in his mouth, which looked frighteningly tight and humorless, and in his eyes, through the narrow vents of which he looked upon his troops with a perpetual look of incredulous distaste. The only curve in the whole design was in his back, which the determined rearward thrust of his shoulders arched in the wrong direction.

There was a relationship between his eyes and his back, between the back thrust of his shoulders and the arrogant forward projection of his chin. All of it was part of a rigid brace, achieved by a simple mechanical means. Lieutenant Jennison wore his helmet liner low in front, so the rim of it came almost down over his eyes. It was only by carrying his shoulders back and his chin high that Lieutenant Jennison could see out from under his pot.

Sergeant Shehan preceded him into the Third Platoon barracks and held the door open for him. Hanson, the acting platoon sergeant, bellowed at the top of his voice, " 'Tetch-HUT!" and every man in the squad room found, by cautious experimentation, that he could brace his shoulders back even farther still.

Andy, and some of the others, watched from the corners of their eyes as the lieutenant began his inspection. One hand hung uselessly by his side; the other held his swagger stick, which prodded irritably among the displays in the foot-locker trays. It pushed and poked, and when it found an item out of place or line it flipped it aside as if it were some small dead reptile.

I wish, Andy said to himself, I had more practice at keeping a room clean.

"Get them head and eyes to the front," Sergeant Shehan said in a low voice to someone, and at least twenty-five sets of head-and-eyes snapped back into position.

The lieutenant stopped in front of Maguire, whose bunk stood next to Andy's, and there was a long and pregnant silence. "The picture on those razor blades," he said with moderated fatigue, "faces the same way as the head of your toothbrush." The swagger stick kicked razor blades and toothbrush aside.

"Suck in that ponderous belly!" said Jennison, and Maguire braced stiffer still.

The lieutenant took a long look at Andy, then stepped forward so that their eyes almost touched. "Did you shine those boots today, soldier?" he demanded.

"Yes, sir," Andy said briskly.

The eyes continued to glare into his. "What the hell with?" said the lieutenant. "A Hershey bar?"

Sergeant Shehan wrote something down in a little black book, and the inspecting party moved on down the line.

"All this webbing," the lieutenant said to the world at large, "has got to be washed at least every other week. And another thing, pertaining to your other gear, rust is very prevailent in this area, so just watch it!"

He was about four bunks down the line by now, which should bring him to either Rodriguez or Hernandez. He stopped, and there was another of those long silences. "Soldier," he said, "were you out there yesterday when I said no damned sideburns in this company?"

"Yes, sir." The voice did not come from either of the Mexicans. It came from Alexander, the sad-looking farm boy.

"All right, then," said the lieutenant. "Get a razor and cut them sideburns off."

"Now, sir?" said Alexander.

"Now!" roared Lieutenant Jennison, sounding as if he were outraged by the question. There was a nervous clatter of equipment in Alexander's foot-locker tray and then the sound of footsteps hurrying toward the latrine.

"Back here!" said Jennison. "I said get a *razor!* I didn't tell you you could use *soap!*"

The inspection of wall lockers was a sobering sight. The swagger stick poked contemptuously into them, pushing the clothing askew. Blouses that were hung facing the wrong way, or blouses from which the brass insignia had not been removed, came out and were held up to the icy view and then were dropped to lie pathetically on the floor.

Then the party went clumping upstairs, and Andy, still holding his brace, felt thankful that it had been no worse. The squad room was littered and messy, which was probably what inspections were for, and the most that they could give him personally was an extra day in the kitchen.

Which was precisely what they gave him.

❖

After the harrowing routines of the past week or more, kitchen police was a surprisingly pleasant, peaceful, relaxing break. Through the foresight of Maguire, who had already begun an analysis and classification of military chores, they managed to get to the potatoes before anyone else thought of it, and they sat on the back steps of the mess hall, leisurely peeling the spuds.

"It's a standard joke among civilians," said Maguire. "They think of a soldier being punished, and the first thing that comes to their minds is peeling potatoes. Do you find the work difficult, distasteful, degrading? No, you do not. The nicest work anywhere in the Army is sitting around like this, taking the hide off an Idaho."

"It's all in your attitude, I suppose," said Andy.

"That," said Maguire, "is the magic word! Attitude! You have to have an open mind. You have to look about you and be on the q.v. at all times. You can decide right at the outset whether you're going to work for the system or let it work for you."

"Say on," said Andy.

"A guy like Hanson will tell you, the first thing you learn in the Army is not to volunteer for *anything.*"

"That makes sense," said Andy.

"It just looks like it makes sense," said Maguire, rather pedagogically. "I look over the situation with a keen scientific eye, and the first thing I see is the value of volunteering. To-night, for example, I'm the CQ runner."

"I'd probably be more impressed," said Andy, "if I knew what a CQ runner was."

"Every night," said Maguire, "some different cadreman is the charge-of-quarters. He sleeps in the orderly room, answers the telephone, wakes up the KPs, puts out the cat. This is a re-sponsible and demanding job, so the CQ needs an assistant to run messages for him and such. That's the CQ runner. It's a modest position of authority, but that's what I volunteered for for tonight."

"Galloping wheelitis," said Andy.

"I got no ambition to be a wheel," said Maguire. "A wheel doesn't go as far as a little can of oil does. That's me, friend—the little can of oil. How long have we been here?"

"Two days, three days."

"Right. And has your old daddy wasted one minute? No, sir. I know more about the work around than half the cadre does. I know the paper work. I know what details to volunteer for and when. At PT this morning, when you were doing those crazy squat-jumps with the others, did you notice where old Maguire was and what he was doing? He was over with the light-duty group, flexing his little old fingers and doing the coordination exercises. While you were sweating, I wasn't even working up a ladylike glow."

"What's your point?" said Andy. "Are you blaming me for not being old and infirm?"

"Of course I am," said Maguire. "Who do you suppose told me to walk over there to the light-duty group? Stormcloud? Lieutenant Taylor? The Army Medical Corps?"

"Who?"

"Me, that's who. I said to myself, Maguire, that's your type of a group. Go over and join them. What I'm trying to tell you, boy, is to use the little gray cells. Think, boy, think!"

"Har de har har," said Andy. "Pardon me, Doctor Einstein. Would you hand me that large potato to the left of your lectern? I can't resist its big brown eyes."

"There's only two things this Army can do to you. It can bluff you, and it can make you mad. It can't get rough with you. It can't make you do push-ups for punishment—"

"Can't make you peel potatoes," said Andy. "This KP bit we're on—that's not punishment, is it?"

"Not legally, it isn't," said Maguire.

"Well, it's a relief to know that."

"Legally this isn't punishment; it's just company duty. There was a job to be done, and they needed somebody to do it, and our names came to their minds because they remembered us from this morning."

"Just coincidence," said Andy.

"Sheaffer," said Maguire, "let me talk to you like a father. You're a brighty boy, and I like the cut of your jib. I hate to see you standing out there in left field. I want to see you shape up, boy. I want to see you get with the group."

"All right," said Andy. "Find me a nice, compatible group. Something civilian."

"Bruce, that model has been discontinued. You better get out and start cranking what you've got. Let me put it this way. You're hip. You know your way around. You didn't go to school just to eat your lunch. So? You get into a situation like this, you let it get under your skin. You walk around with your lip hanging out. You get mad when they give you a haircut. You get mad because you don't like the drape of your threads. You jaw back at the turnkeys. If the sign in the latrine says don't throw butts in the urinal, you have to throw butts in the urinal. You get into a situation that you're not going to get out of for at least two years, come hell or however, and what do you do? Do you look around and make yourself comfortable? No. Not you. You go ape!"

"Let's go with those potatoes!" someone yelled from the kitchen.

"All you need," said Maguire, "is the one simple motto, which is: Easy, Greasy, it's a long slide. Cool down, slack off, and you know what you'll have?"

"Tell me, doctor."

"You'll have the best thing in life: no sweat."

It hit Andy unexpectedly and left him confused. My Lord, he said to himself, that's *my* line.

❖

Maguire is right, Andy reflected as he ambled toward the supply room on an errand for the mess steward. Relax is the key word; relax and enjoy it.

How did I get this keyed up and irritable? he asked himself, and why does it stay so long? I walk in with a wild hair worrying at me, and I inquire around for trouble, and who needs trouble? The easiest bit on the whole card is Getting Along with the Group, and look whose little boy is flubbing it.

If I could just get five minutes all to myself, to go off to one side and cool down—but who gets five minutes for anything around this cokey outfit? These characters, snapping at my hindquarters twenty-four hours a day . . .

Newly irritated by this thought, he took the cigarette from his mouth and flipped it off his thumb into the street.

This was as far as he got in his meditations. At that very second the stillness of the company street was neatly torn through by a small but ominous sound: the clearing of the military throat. A voice—not a loud one, but one that crackled as with static electricity—reached out and struck him solidly between the shoulder blades.

"Soldier!"

Andy turned and saw the stiff figure and the prim, professorial, unsmiling face of the first sergeant. The sergeant's finger slowly drew a horizontal circle in the air, soared aloft some twelve inches or so, and plummeted down into the center of it. Andy walked over and placed himself, not precisely in the spot indicated, but reasonably close to it.

"What's your name?" Hanna demanded.

"Sheaffer," said Andy. "Sir."

"You have just come to a turning point in your military career," said the sergeant. "A wise recruit never gives his first sergeant or his company commander any occasion to know that he even exists. You have made your first large mistake in the Army."

"Yes, sir," said Andy.

"I have just witnessed two offenses of a serious nature. First, I have seen a recruit in my own company traveling at a walk, instead of double-timing as he is instructed to. The second offense is a serious one for any soldier on the post or anywhere else in the Army."

"Sir?" said Andy.

"You disposed of a cigarette in the company street without field-stripping it. The Army is very fussy about things of that nature, and it has damned good reason to be. We have two hundred and thirty-seven men in this company alone, and that doesn't leave any room for hogs and litterbugs. Is that clear?"

"Yes, sir."

"Pick it up," said Hanna.

Andy retrieved the cigarette from the asphalt and stood there holding it between his middle finger and thumb.

"Unwrap it," said the sergeant. "Now drop the tobacco in the street and scatter it with your foot. Now wad the paper into a tiny ball and put it in your pocket. Now what have you got?"

"The beaverboard, sir," said Andy, holding up the filter.

"Put that in your other pocket," said the sergeant. Andy did. "Was that procedure difficult or easy?"

"Easy, sir," said Andy.

"The next time I see you flipping butts in the street," said the first sergeant, "we're going to do it the hard way. The next time you're going to pick that gasper up and bury it. You will dig a hole six by six by six feet deep, where the wind will not blow it back to offend my sight."

"Yes, sir."

"In the hardest, rockiest ground I can find for you to dig. And when you've finished disposing of the butt we will have a thorough discussion of your attitude in general. Is *that* clear?"

"Yes, sir."

"All right, Sheaffer. Pick up your feet, high and fast, and continue where you were going. The next time I see you wandering around, I want you to be double-timing and sounding off until hell won't have it. Take off!"

Andy took off, trotting and roaring. The first sergeant stood there looking after him with flinty speculation.

six

"This," said Andy Sheaffer, "is my rifle. There are many like it, but this one is mine."

Andy's voice was one of some two hundred voices united in the ritual chant. In an area next to regimental headquarters, under the sharp eyes of Colonel Marcus A. F. Whippet, the trainees of Fox Company were sounding off in the Rifleman's Creed. Each clutched in his hands an item he had personally received from the hands of the colonel himself: eighty-eight dollars' worth of Clip-Fed, Gas-Operated, Air-Cooled, Semi-Automatic Shoulder Weapon, U. S. Caliber .30, M-1. The re-sounding nomenclature of the weapon had been drilled into their drowsy heads by instructors from the division faculty. The price of the piece was easier to remember; it was clearly sten-ciled in white paint on the stock of each rifle.

"My rifle is my best friend," said the two hundred-odd voices. "I will protect my rifle and it will protect me. Together we will protect my country."

That, in effect, finished off the rifle-presentation ceremony, although a few trifling side details remained to be attended to. The interval between the men in the formation was a rather close one, and when they were given Left Face some of the shouldered rifles clattered against some of the others, and more than one man had to duck quickly to avoid being brained.

The colonel was at this very moment commenting upon this unfortunate circumstance to the company commander. The latter would pass his criticisms and suggestions on to Sergeant

Hanna, who in turn would address himself to Sergeant Storm-cloud, who would have a few words with his platoon sergeants, and by the time the results trickled down to Enlisted Grade No. 1 (recruits), Colonel Whippet's quiet words would have attained a seven-fold amplification. Furthermore, many men would be available for extra little chores around the place the next day.

It was as Cadreman Clyde had defined it back in the service unit: *They chew me, and I chew you. This is the Law of the Jungle.*

Well, Andy reflected, back in the barracks, the dice have hit the backboard and thus they fall. He expressed this sentiment to Henry Carleton, who sat on the neighboring bunk, thoughtfully rubbing the stock of his rifle.

"I tell you!" said Carleton. "These people got a system, like everybody else. I think, once I get caught up on my sleep, I'm not going to have any trouble with these people. I'll find the way they like it done, and I'll do it their way."

"No sweat," said Andy.

"No sweat," said Carleton.

Hanson, the acting platoon sergeant, came out of his room at the end of the barracks and paused beside them.

"Let's cut the crap," said Hanson, "and be putting them rifles away. Sheaffer, are you chewing gum?"

"That I am, sergeant sir," said Andy.

"May I ask what the hell you did with the wrapper?"

"Why?" said Andy.

"Because," said Hanson, "I'm getting tired of finding these little souvenirs of yours all over the place."

"I've got the wrapper in my pocket," said Andy. "When the taste has fled the chicle, I intend to wrap it in the paper before disposing of said. Isn't that military?"

"All right," Hanson said tiredly. "But in the butt can—or in the trash. Not on the latrine floor, like this morning."

"I'm pitifully sorry," said Andy. "You see, I've never had roommates before."

Hanson snorted mildly. "That's for damned sure," he said.

❖

Slowly, almost sneakily, Andrew Sheaffer was beginning to relax and feel his way about. He vaguely noticed that some of the others in the platoon were taking things easier. McGregor, one of the men upstairs, who had trouble distinguishing left from right, was sentenced to carry a rock in his left hand all morning, and he did it blithely.

Andy himself, forgetting to sound his "Here, sir!" loud and clear, was forced to double-time once around a barracks, shouting "Here, sir!" at every step. Making the circuit, he was astonished to find that he was laughing as loudly as the others.

He had no real idea, though, of how easy it was becoming for him until one morning at breakfast, early in the second week, when Hernandez spilled a cup of coffee on the mess-hall floor. It could have happened to any of them, for all were still awkward from lack of sleep, and from tension, and from general nervousness.

Hernandez, having loaded his tray at the serving counter, had crossed dazedly over to the forty-gallon pot in front of the icebox, where a KP with a dipper poured the coffee into his cup. Hernandez had just started for a table when someone slammed the icebox door, at least six feet behind him. The boy's twitch shook his tray, and the coffee cup jumped off it and crashed to the floor.

Andy, at the nearest table, was startled by the noise. He saw first the cup, lying in its pool of coffee, and then the face of the boy who had dropped it. Hernandez stood rigid, seemingly paralyzed with shock and terror. It was as if a finger from heaven had suddenly pointed him out for quick and terrible destruction. He stood there like that until the mess steward,

Sergeant Hofeller, perturbed by the sight, came over and patted his arm several times and told him to get himself another cup.

Throughout the morning the boy seemed still pale and shaky, and Andy found it difficult to push the panicked face out of his mind. A week ago, he said to himself, that is precisely the way I would have reacted if I had dropped the coffee. I'm not afraid of anything these people can do.

Given an occasional chance at relaxation and reflection, such as the minutes he spent perched on the barracks overhang, washing the second-story windows, he was able to see progress in himself. Except for the physical strain—the fatigue, the lack of sleep—there was nothing difficult about this whole military bit. From map-reading to guard duty, from lectures on how to salute automobiles to demonstrations of how to get out from under the bleachers when they opened the can of tear gas, it was all like everything else: a snap. Even the way he was doing it himself, with the first sergeant's cold, bespectacled eyes upon him, and the Field First giving him an extra dose of personal attention, there was nothing to it.

Strangely enough, the military routine was less difficult than the purely social, the bit that to him should have been no more than a walk-on. There were strange characters in the platoon, men with all sorts of backgrounds and prejudices and little resentments that winced when touched. He was learning not to mention well-known people in his civilian circle of acquaintance, or places he had been where some of the others might not have been, or things he owned that they did not. Say something without thinking, something that means nothing at all, and suddenly there is the funny little look on someone's face. Real life, he reflected, had never been like this.

He would watch his step, though, and he would have no trouble. No sweat.

❖

Sometimes of an evening, tired of the voices of Maguire and the others, tired of their very nearness, he would sit on the back steps after Lights Out, smoking a birdwood and thinking.

Hanson, he noticed, used the same time for walking; sometimes he would pause on his way back into the barracks and sit for a while, usually with silence and a thoughtful loneliness.

As acting platoon sergeant, George Hanson walked a narrow line between his trainee status and his simulated rank. He had stoutly protested the latter, arguing that he was too old and slow to lead a platoon of hearty teen-agers.

"You're no older than I am," Hanna had said. "There's a chronic shortage of noncoms around here, and when I find a qualified man I've got no patience with modesty. You're taking the Third Platoon."

"If that's the way it is," Hanson had said, and Stormcloud had helped to pin the brassard around his sleeve.

The Third Platoon found him quiet but firm, humorless but sympathetic. As a veteran he knew the responsibility he had taken; as a new inductee he knew the feelings and the problems of his men.

"I'm not supposed to cuss at these people," he said to Andy one evening as they sat together smoking on the back steps, "but if I had the talent I sure would use it. It's pitiful how little harassing they have to get by on."

"Why *more* harassing?" said Andy. "Because that's the way they did it in the Old Army?"

"They knew what they were doing," said Hanson. "The way they do it now, you're going to come out of the Army just as soft and civilian as you went in."

"That's what I'm hoping for," said Andy. "I'm not looking to this Army to teach me a trade."

"You're looking to them to make a soldier out of you," said Hanson, "in case they need one in a hurry. And this ain't the way to do it. They're supposed to toughen you up inside and out, and one's just as important as the other. They can harden your hide by just running it ragged, and when they finish, you'll look like a soldier. That's not going to callus you inside, though. The only way to do that is by hollering and cussing and making you think like a grownup. That's the way they did it when I first went in, and I enjoyed it a damned sight more than I do this. I felt like I was getting something for my money."

Andy looked at him with some astonishment. "That's a long speech," he said.

"Long time thinking about it," said Hanson. They sat thinking a long time before Hanson spoke up again. "There's a division over in those new concrete barracks," he said, "where the captain had to apologize to the men for telling them a dirty story. Wasn't even very dirty, at that. Some boy wrote his mother, and she wrote the colonel over there. Colonel made the captain apologize. Isn't that something?"

Andy felt a sudden, unaccustomed surge of compassion for the older man. "You've got a real crush on this stinking old institution, haven't you?"

"I haven't got a crush on *anything*," said Hanson, "but I'm comfortable here. I was out of it for ten years, and I wasn't comfortable out there at all. When I'm in the Army I feel like I'm doing something with my time." He looked off down the quiet street. "Isn't that humorous?"

Andy shrugged tolerantly. "Different people," he said, "have different ways of getting their jollies. Live, love, laugh, and be happy."

"What do *you* want to get out of the Army?" said Hanson.

"Me," said Andy.

"Those are the kind of answers I wish I could think of," said Hanson. There was a hint of reproach in his voice. "All right, let me give you another one, just because I'm curious.

You're a different age, and you grew up different than me. What have you got a crush on?"

"A girl, sometimes," said Andy. "That's nice and pleasant and out of the high-rent district. I'm lucky, daddy-o. I don't go around getting enthusiastic about things."

"Why would that be?"

"There's damned little that's worth it," said Andy, "and damned little that costs that much. I don't have to get enthusiastic about anything, especially something like the Army. I can do anything they've got, and do it in a breeze."

"You're not doing anything in any breeze."

"The hell I'm not. They had me rattled for a while, but I'm back on my feet. I've got the beat and I'm going to ride with it easy."

Hanson rose and stretched himself. "I'm going to flake out for the night," he said. "You got all your gear marked for tomorrow? Inspection's at ten-thirty."

"Sure," said Andy. "Always prepared."

They parted genially, neither of them suspecting that this would be the last note of cordiality between them for many days to come.

The Third Platoon was gigged in the inspection the next morning. This meant that for a whole week it would be the "rout-step" platoon of the company, placed at the bottom of the chow line and given first priority for all the dirty little jobs around the area.

The platoon had deserved it. Lieutenant Taylor, inspecting the barracks, had found a candy wrapper under one of the bunks.

Sheaffer's bunk, to be precise.

The rest of it was not Andy's fault at all. He had no part of it, he knew nothing about it, and he would have been appalled at the thought that such a thing could happen.

As of noon that Thursday no one could have picked the most popular man in the Third Platoon, but there was no question who was the best-known member of it, the man uppermost in the thoughts of his fellows. Some of the men were seriously discussing a plan to extend to Andrew J. Sheaffer that most effective of all trainee gestures—a GI shower, with yellow soap and brushes.

Then came the other. The divinity which shapes our ends reached out and cut a large slice off Andrew Sheaffer's.

It was late afternoon in the orderly room when Corporal Goldberg, the company clerk, reached across his desk and raised the little window that gave into the company commander's office. "Sir," he said, "it's Long Distance. Person-to-person to the Commanding Officer." He gave a neat little flourish to the resounding title.

Lieutenant Jennison looked over at Lieutenant Taylor, who was leaning against his portable phonograph. The machine was playing, in cautiously muted tones, "Gems from *The Student Prince*."

"Could I pervade upon you to turn that damn thing off?" said the company commander. When the order had been carried out—with ill grace—he picked up the phone and spoke into it. "Lieutenant Jennison, sir!"

The "sir" at the other end of the line was a crisp and cultured female voice. "I am Mrs. Arthur Sheaffer of West Los Angeles," it said. "My son, Andrew Sheaffer, is a member of your organization, I believe."

"One moment, ma'am," said Lieutenant Jennison. He rolled his eyes wearily for Lieutenant Taylor's benefit, placed his hand over the mouthpiece, and yelled into the first sergeant's office. "Sergeant Hanna! We got a Sheaffer in this outfit?"

"I'm afraid we have," the sergeant replied. "He's the playboy up in the Third Platoon."

"That's correct, ma'am," Jennison said into the telephone.

"I wonder if it would be at all possible," said Mrs. Sheaffer, "for him to come home for two or three days."

"I'm sorry, ma'am," said the lieutenant. "We don't give any passes during the first four weeks of training."

It was doubtful that Madeline heard or heeded more than half of the latter sentence. "Is there a sensible reason for this," she asked, "or is it just another of those Army traditions?"

Lieutenant Jennison was considerably irritated by her tone but too well trained in contemporary command functions to make a point of it. "There's a very practical reason, ma'am. If your son misses three consectional days of training, he falls back to another training company whose schedule is a week behind ours. They don't usually prefer to retergrade like that. So unless there's a very urgent reason—"

"As a matter of fact," said Mrs. Sheaffer, "there is. Do weekends count on that consecutive business?"

"No, ma'am."

"Good. Now, it happens that we are negotiating a very important transfer of stock in my husband's publishing business, and I'm afraid that Private Sheaffer's presence is essential to the transaction."

This is a new one, the lieutenant said to himself as he put his hand over the mouthpiece again. Taylor looked up at him. "Here we go," said Jennison. "Starting early. This one wants a three-day pass for a third-week man. Hey, Hanna!" The first sergeant came to the door of the office. "Can we give one of these suntan civilians a pass over the weekend—if he's got a good and sufficient pretext?"

"It's your company, Lieutenant," said Hanna. "Under the provisions of SR 600-115-10, Leaves and Passes, it so states that leaves may be granted at the discretion of the company commander."

"They need this Sheaffer back home for some big financial deal. What do you think? Give him the pass?"

"Why, hell yes," said the first sergeant. "What's good for General Motors is good for Company F."

"Mrs. Sheaffer," said Jennison, "I think we can arrange it. We'll get him out first thing in the morning. . . . You're extremely welcome, ma'am."

He laid down the telephone and looked up at the first sergeant. "What the hell are you grinning about?"

"Just thinking, lieutenant," said Hanna. "One less man to train. Third Platoon will train this one for me."

❖

The farthest he got in the direction of Los Angeles was the telephone center next door to the service club. He set his little A-wol bag on the floor, twisted himself into a booth, and put the call through, station-to-station, collect.

"Mother," he said when they had got rid of the operator.

"Darling!" said Madeline.

"What's the emergency, Mother?"

Her laugh was gay and tinkly. "There isn't any emergency, sweetie!"

"What's all this about papers to sign and stocks to transfer? I don't know anything about any stocks."

"Of *course* you don't, dear. That's all April Fool!" Then, across the lengthening silence: "Andrew! Are you still there?"

"I'm here," said Andy.

"I was so lonesome for you," said Madeline, "and you've been away *such* a long time! So I took things in my own hands! Aren't you glad?"

"Mother," he said slowly, "let me get it straight. There isn't any emergency—or anything?"

"Don't be silly!" She laughed. "It's all a wonderful scheme to get you home for a day or two. It's a *surprise!*"

"God," said Andy.

"Sweetheart," she said, "I've checked all the plane schedules, because the train is just impossibly slow. Now, there's a flight out of Esperanza at nine-thirty that will get you into International before eleven, and I'll meet you there."

"Mother," he said, "I'm not coming."

"What on earth are you talking about?" said Madeline. "You have a three-day pass!"

"It would take a long time to explain," he said, "but I don't want a three-day pass!"

"Andrew!" Her tone was one of bewilderment and hurt.

"Mother, I'm in the Army. I'm in a company with two hundred men, and all of us are supposed to be stuck right where we are. How do you think they feel when one gets a pass and the rest don't? They feel damned unfriendly."

This time it was Madeline who was silent. Then: "You sound as if I'd done you a disservice."

"You could say that, Mother."

"Put you in Coventry?"

"Yes, Mother."

"It was done with the very best intentions."

"All right, Mother."

"And you're positively not coming home?"

"No, Mother."

"Very well," she said. "I'm sorry, Andrew." And then, more brightly: "I'm sure it's going to be all right. They're having that Open House thing up there next weekend, and you'll be feeling better then. We'll talk about it when your father and I come up."

"I'd rather you didn't," said Andy. "Come up next week, I mean. I'd like a little longer to get feeling better."

❖

At first glance, the simplest thing to do would be to hike the short distance back to Fox Company, turn in his pass at the orderly room, and inconspicuously resume his place in ranks. This was not the simple solution, though; this was only the ideal solution.

How would one comport himself, traveling the long and open company street, climbing the steps to that unfriendly bastion: Knock and Remove Cap before Entering? Standing before Hanna's desk, nervously fluttering the unused pass in one hand, looking into the first-soldier's peculiarly bleak and knowing eyes, how would one begin the conversation?

I'm sorry to have put you to the trouble, sergeant; it was kind of you to give me the pass, but I really cannot accept it. My mother is an impulsive woman, sergeant, and not accustomed to our Army ways and thought. This talk of stocks and papers to sign, these are the products of an agile and whimsical mind. If you have ever had a mother, sergeant, I'm sure you'll understand. Laugh at her playful foibles, and forgive.

Brother, that would be the day.

There was a taxicab station next to the telephone center, and he slid into the back seat of a hack. A driver came out of the building and took his place behind the wheel. "What'll it be?" he asked Andy.

"Friend," said Andy, "where would a man get a drink at this time of day?"

"Place out on the San Fidel Road," said the driver. "It's where the sergeants hang out. Rannahan's We-Never-Close. You want that one?"

"Sure," said Andy. "Why not? Why the hell not?"

The place was empty, except for one bartender and a few people halfheartedly tidying it up. There was nothing to do but sit and nurse a drink. Andy saw two double scotches through the crisis and wandered out again.

Hitchhiking here and there, taking a taxicab occasionally to break the pace, he roamed restlessly about the area, finding nothing because he had no idea what he wanted to find.

There was nowhere to go around here, nothing to do, except to prowl about aimlessly and let his radiator boil.

seven

THE SIGHTSEEING BUS offered, at the very least, a place to sit and be left alone for two or three hours, so Andy gave the driver a dollar and climbed aboard. In time the bus filled and started off, working its way through San Fidel and out along the shoreline.

It had made no more than two or three stops when he discovered that he did not want to sit—at least, not here. He was annoyed by the sights pointed out to him, the relics of questionable historic interest; he was annoyed by the bored voice of the driver, slapping relentlessly at him from a loudspeaker. He was most particularly annoyed by the enforced company of forty or more faces, none of which he liked.

It was almost time for the next inevitable stop when he saw a quiet, isolated strip of coast that seemed to beckon him, a place where great spines of rock ran out into the sea and the sand formed shallow little laps in the crevices between them.

A little farther on, the bus stopped again, disgorging its two-score culture-lovers before a rocky shrine, a place where an Indian maiden had done something or other in the dim but unforgotten past. While the others adjusted their cameras, and bought their relics, and pointed things out to one another,

Andy detached himself from the group and started walking back in the direction from which they had come.

After a mile or so he came upon the place he had seen from the bus window. He climbed a point of rock and followed it out to the end, where he sat and glowered at the sea. Somewhere in the morning's travels he had providently purchased a bottle and stowed it, wrapped in a bath towel, in his A-wol bag. Now he dragged it out and laid it on the rock beside him, and suddenly he felt that he had, after all, a friend.

He lifted the bottle to his lips and took a long, thoughtful swig at it. It was a very smooth scotch whisky, and he was soon feeling a little smoother himself. The noise of the waves against the rocks had been somehow truculent before; now it became mellow and congenial.

The highway was out of sight above and behind him, and the infrequent cars that passed made only a distant and impersonal sound. He and the bottle enjoyed the peace and solitude.

Sometime later, somewhere in the back of his mind, it seemed as if he heard a car stopping on the highway back there, and then the slamming of a door, but he did not bother to turn and look. But then he became aware that there was life on one of the little beaches below. A healthy-looking, clean-limbed girl carrying a beach towel was striding down toward the water, swinging her very blond hair out of her face as she came. She threw down the towel, shucked out of her dress, and flung it down beside the towel. She stood for a moment, shapely and magnificent in a pale blue two-piece bathing suit; then she plowed out into the rough, cold water and disappeared into a breaker.

"They're rationing the privacy now," Andy said to the bottle. "Little buddy, somebody's found Our Place."

He set the bottle down to rest and watched the girl sporting about far out in the water, and then he began to puzzle whether he and his friend were intruding upon her private preserve, or she upon theirs, or contrariwise. If it were true, 'twere pity, and, pity 'tis, 'tis true. He spent some time trying to remember where he had heard that line (or something like it) before, and by the time he had given up he felt a little better. By that time, too, the girl was emerging from the sea.

By George, she was a stunning creature. What was it that they used to say in school? Eyeballs, come back here!

Eyeballs, he said, you really shouldn't be here at all.

The towel, it developed, was two: the large one for the sand, and a small one in which she wrapped the dazzling hair. She stretched out on the beach towel, yawned happily, and suddenly sat up. She was reaching to unhook her halter when Andy decided to do something about the situation.

"Don't do it, friend!" he shouted. "There might be people about!"

The sudden sound startled her, and then she looked around to find where it came from. Shading her eyes, she finally saw him on the rock above.

The whole thing felt a little silly to him, but his voice was neighborly. "Big Brother is watching you!"

"Soldier," she said with philosophic impersonality, "why does this sort of thing always happen?"

"It's just that kind of day," said Andy. "I can climb down the far side of this crag and get lost if you like—or find another crag. I know exactly how you feel."

"You don't have to," said the girl. "When you went, somebody else would come barging along. Keep your seat." Then, as an afterthought: "What are you doing up there?"

"Sitting," he said. "And thinking. And drinking."

"Like that," said the girl. "All right, I'll go away."

"No," he said. "Then I'd feel bad about it."

"Well, come on down," she called. "And bring your bottle."

❖

It was much later, in somebody's apartment.

"What happened?" said Andy. "All of a sudden?"

"Yep," she said, "all of a something. We were going great. We were getting stiff in every joint, isn't that funny? And then, wham, bam, the ax fell. All we did, we just ran out of saloons."

"You're a very beautiful woman," said Andy. "You're a magnificent woman. What did you say your name was? Is?"

"Maggi," she said. "I told you. Maggi Van Kleef."

"Maggi Van Kleef," he said judiciously. "And that's a very lovely name. Maggi."

"Mad Margaret," said Maggi.

"Where are we now?" said Andy. "The snows of yesteryear. What place is this?"

"This is home," said Maggi. "Where we have breakfast."

"What time is it?"

"It is six o'clock of a Friday afternoon. Best time there is for breakfast."

"A noble time," said Andy. "Stately."

She gave him ham and eggs and a lot of coffee, and then he began to brood.

"What?" said Maggi.

"That's going to spoil everything," he said. "It has already. I think I'm going to be sober."

"You have that sad look," she said, "even when you're not sober."

"Moody boy," said Andy. "It's a gypsy strain somewhere. This is an awfully wide sofa for two people."

Laughing, she moved over next to him. He ran his fingers pensively up and down the side of her neck, and then they came together in a long kiss.

"Moody," she said, rising. "And sober too. The one before had a lot more feeling."

"Six o'clock?" he asked, as if he were having difficulty getting it clear.

"That's all. You want to take a nap? You don't. All right, then. We'll start all over. You know what's in the icebox?"

"Ice?"

"A large bottle of bubbly. Saving it to celebrate something. Maybe it would make us feel celebrative."

"With stout," said Andy. "You don't have stout?"

"No stout."

"I could get some," he said, "if I were in any condition to drive."

"Walk," said Maggi. "Down to the corner."

He put his cap on, backward, and she changed it for him, and he started out.

"How much stout?" he asked at the door.

"One bottle," said Maggi. "We've got only one bottle of bubbly." While he stood there, considering this, she crossed to him, straightened his necktie, patted his shoulder, and looked as if she were going to say something. Instead she gave him a fond and almost maternal kiss and sped him off.

The evening was still early, and there was champagne left in the bottle, when he laid his head in her lap and fell fast asleep.

With difficulty she managed to get him out of his uniform and wrap him in a blanket on the sofa.

❖

On Saturday she took him out for a game of golf, and then they went swimming in the little cove where they had met. On Saturday night they got a little drunk again. "It's silly," Maggi said, "but I don't know what else I can do with you."

"Let me be very sober for a minute," said Andy. "Let me say that I'm mad about you. You are the pink, pink limit."

"Good old Maggi," she said a little wistfully. "I'm mad about you too, fellow."

"A fine ironical tone," said Andy.

"I'm a fine ironical girl." She ran her fingers through the stubble of his hair.

"Suppose I finish the drink," said Andy, "and as silently steal away."

"No," she said. "I'll behave. You're going to stay right here. I want to count your drinks and keep you out of trouble."

"Trouble?"

"You have the look again. You're lonesome for trouble, and looking for it. If you have to have it, look at me and pretend I'm trouble. Usually I am."

Andy looked at her: the strong, perfect face, the shimmery blond hair, the hint of a little droop in the magnificent shoulders. Here is one, he said, as moody as anyone I've ever seen. Except that she carries it well.

"You're a good kid," he said. "A very good kid."

"Aren't I, though?" said Maggi. "I think that's one of my problems." Then, tenderly: "What are your problems like?"

"Just problems."

"One of them's a girl," she said suddenly.

"I don't know," said Andy. "I don't have a girl."

"That makes it one-sided," said Maggi. "Some girl's got you."

"Will you be my girl?" said Andy.

"Sure," she said. "While you need me. Rich, ripe, fun-loving Van Kleef."

eight

FROM THE MAGUIRE PAPERS:

146. Sunday evening. The Army is slipping. No harassing, no all out cleaning of barracks. Somebody goofed, forgot to call an inspection for Mon. morning. Heads will roll for this.

147. Sheaffer has shifted position. Still has his head in a bag, but now also his tail in a sling. Troops restless about his 3 day pass for big financial deal. Muttering more now, rumor says was no such deal in first place.

148. Persons with phys. infirmity can get Light Duty slip for as much 3 days at a time. Bad back is shrewdest bet. Army cant find the pain, cant say you havent got it. Light Duty with bad back means no pack carrying, no double timing, no Phys. Training. Check further.

149. Out to rifle range tomorrow for the whole week. Firing M-1 for record. Consulted with Polier abt helping him with master score sheet, but he plans to grope his way thru it without expert assistance from me. Try volunteering for ammo detail. This means stacking brass, taking ammo out, keeping firing line ready, and distribute equipmt. A good deal, but work involved. Ammo detail sleeps in barracks while their comrades are roughing it on bivouack. . . .

Range guards for towers sit around doing nothing but answering phone evy ½ hr and reporting any flying aircraft or ships at sea. Flake out on the floor and enjoy life. . . . Who will be driving the trucks?

150. Being a medic is a good deal, but you have to be a medic to be one. If a man was to get hold of a clip board and pencil, and walk around making notes, nobody would bother him and he would not get sore muscles. Must try this.

151. Co. commander improving his vocabulary evy day. Overheard him saying to 1st Sgt. yesterday, I dont know what regt hq. wants, they say one thing and then turn right around and counteract themselves.

152. A fleet footed courier from the orderly room reports A. J. Sheaffer is at this moment checking in from his 3 day pass. News is making the natives restless all over again. As pityous as my own plight, I thank whatever Gods there be at least I am not A. J. Sheaffer.

Signing off now to get out the 1st aid kit.

❖

First Sergeant Hanna, cool and casual in a T-shirt, sat at the typewriter in his office, apparently catching up with his personal correspondence. "If that's Sheaffer," he called out into the orderly room, "I want to see him."

All right, said Andy, let him do his damnedest. He finished signing in in the sign-out book and moved into the first sergeant's presence. "Private Sheaffer, sir," he said.

Hanna typed out three or four more words before he looked up. "You'd better get yourself over to the telephone center," he said, "and put in a call to LA. Your mother's called two or three dozen times, and she sounds real worried."

"Yes, sir," said Andy.

"She doesn't understand you the way we do," said Hanna. Andy felt himself reddening. The sergeant turned back to his typewriter, as if he considered the interview ended.

"That's all?" said Andy.

"What do you want?" said Hanna. "A silver loving cup? Take off."

Andy stood there, awkward and undecided. One thing was certain, although he could not say why: the thing could not be left hanging here. "Sergeant," he said, "I think I could explain if I had the chance."

"Don't explain anything to me," said Hanna. "I don't need any explanation. I don't want any. Any time you can pull yourself a shrewdie, you go ahead and do it. It's no skin off my bottom."

His face was so mellow and tolerant, his voice so quiet, that Andrew Sheaffer felt an overwhelming desire to smash his fist into the middle of the smile. He held himself stiff, and clenched his teeth, and pulled himself together. "I haven't tried to pull a shrewdie," he said, going very slowly and carefully. "The whole thing was not altogether my fault."

"Of course not," said Hanna. "You're modern youth. You're society's fault. Close the door, Sheaffer."

Andy closed the door.

"You've won this decision," said Hanna. "You've outfoxed the Army. You've had yourself a little holiday that nobody else had. Don't expect *me* to get into a lather over it. It didn't cost me a nickel.

"You haven't lost a lot either, Sheaffer, except a few friends, and I don't think you'll come unglued over a trifle like that. You missed a little M-1 instruction and a rifle-coaches' class, but you're the type to pick that up real quick. And if you don't, so what. Eh?"

"What happens now?" said Andy.

"You mean," said the sergeant, "am I going to ream you for this, make life hard for you? No, Sheaffer, I'm not. I haven't got the time. I've got two hundred and thirty-seven men in this company. If I give *any* of them personal attention it's going to be the ones that are worth it, the ones I think I can do something with."

"I don't follow you," said Andy.

"I don't think you ever will," said Hanna, "so I'm not going into a spin about it. I don't like your attitude, and I never have, and I never will—but it's your attitude, sonny, and your problem. You're just a light operator."

"Thank you very much," said Andy, the outrage boiling inside him.

"Now, one thing about your attitude is this. You've got it in your head somewhere that you're doing prison time or something. You act like we're paid to persecute you or something. Well, disabuse yourself, Jack. You're one man in a million and a quarter, and nobody gives a damn whether you get properly persecuted or not. We're only supposed to make a soldier out of you. You can grasp that, can't you?"

"Yes, sir."

"There are some people that hell and hard labor couldn't make soldiers out of, and you look like one of that group to me. I've got three qualified cadremen in this company to do the work of twenty-three instructors. I've got twenty trainees keeping one page ahead of the people they're training. There's not a damned one of them got the time to blow your nose or take you to the bathroom."

"Sergeant," said Andy.

"I'm talking, mister," said Hanna, "and don't you rattle till I tell you to. We've got a lot of people here not a bit happier than you are about being drug into the Army, but they take it the way they're supposed to, and they try to learn what we try to teach. They've found out somewhere they're not required to like it; they're just required to do it. Those are the ones on the way to growing up.

"I don't know who you were on the outside, or what you had, and I can't say I give a damn. But somewhere you've got the idea that this is a hell of an imposition on you, and you're too big for this kind of a deal. You're not big enough, Jack. You're out of your speed around here."

He stopped there, and sat back looking at Andy—not emotionally, not even curiously, but merely reflectively.

"Is that all?" said Andy, when the warmth in his own face became uncomfortable.

"That's all, Sheaffer," said the sergeant. "You go back to your barracks, and pretend there's nobody else there. As far as basic training is concerned, just go your merry way the way you've been going. Do as little as you can get by with, and get away with everything you can. You're not missing anything when you miss the military. If anything ever comes up, you'll slide through one way or another."

"Very well, sir," Andy said stiffly.

"And, Sheaffer," said the first sergeant, "you don't have to 'sir' me in private. Only when there are soldiers around!"

❖

Up at four o'clock that morning, it seemed almost like the first week of training again, when four had been the standard time for rising. Nobody had much to say to Sheaffer; everybody, for that matter, seemed to be carefully avoiding him. Pushing his breakfast tray toward the coffee can, he wondered where he could eat this morning, and with whom.

Midway up the dining room he saw Carleton alone at a table, thoughtfully staring at the French toast before him. When Andy eased into the chair opposite him, Carleton looked up at him briefly and then back down at the toast. His manner was not aggressively rude. It was only disinterested.

There was a certain amount of clatter as Ransom Maguire set his tray down on the vacant side of the table. He studied the tray as if he were taking inventory, looked all about him at the breakfast crowd, and finally sat down. "At ease, men," he said.

"Hey, Ransom," said Carleton, "I thought you were the number-one scuffle-worker in this unit. How come you can't promote things like Sheaffer can promote things? You're no wheel, Bruce. You're just a plain old hubcap."

"Put an egg in your shoe," said Maguire, "and beat it."

"One thing my mamma always told me," said Carleton, "was it's those quiet ones you've got to watch. Next to old Sheaffer here, you know what you are? You are a gas-operated, air-cooled, semi-automatic propaganda man."

Andy doggedly addressed himself to his breakfast. Maguire smiled benevolently through his horn-rims at Carleton. "You grow on me," he said. "Like fungus."

"I'm going to save it," said Carleton, "for the next outfit I'm in. I'm going to tell them loud and clear. My family is buying up some railroads this week, and they need me around to tell them which ones. How are these people going to know whether I'm the country-club element or not?"

❖

Fox was to spend the first half of the week in the pits, pulling targets for Dog Company. On Wednesday afternoon Dog Company would move into the pits and Fox Company would take over the firing line.

The firing was to begin promptly at seven; at six-thirty they were on the range and ready to go. An officer in charge of the pit details instructed them, slowly and methodically, on the handling of the targets. He gave them their assignments—two men on each target, twenty men on the phones—and they galloped off to the sheds to draw their equipment.

Carleton and Sheaffer were assigned to pull the target at Point 31. The latter took this as an indication that his luck was still running bad. Of all the men in the company, Carleton was the one he least wanted to be next to for all this uncomfortable week. The company was full of men he did not know or did not particularly like, and he would have vastly preferred to have been teamed with some relative stranger. Carleton was too close a friend, and far too disapproving. With someone else, it would not have mattered.

Together, silently, they hoisted the huge target into its frame; then Carleton checked the pulley and the counterweights. Andy hefted and examined the pointer—a twelve-foot pole with a disk at each end, to be raised up in front of the target to show the location and the value of the hit. He tested the edge of a disk against his thumb and whistled.

"Cha!" he said to Carleton, hoping to start a conversation. "You notice how sharp these are? I'll bet this would go right through my helmet."

Carleton made no reply, but he looked as if he thought it not a bad idea.

The nearby loudspeaker suddenly roared, "When you've got your equipment and your targets in, raise your targets!"

Together they hoisted the target. Then Carleton sat down on the bench across from it, his back to the firing line, and looked as if he were completely alone in the long ten-by-ten trench. For a second Andy thought of sitting down beside him, but he decided against it. He looked up the line to a point near the center, where some of the cadre had started a fire. Beside it sat Maguire, who had found the detail he wanted. He had no target, no telephone; he was in charge of looking after Lieutenant Taylor's phonograph.

"Henry," Andy said to Carleton, "what are you bugging me for? What have I done to you?"

"You haven't did nothing to me," said Carleton.

"So why am I all of a sudden the black widow around here? How come you got a sudden urge to short my sheets?"

"I just been looking at you, friend," said Carleton, "and you don't show me much."

"Firing will commence!" shouted the squawk-box. "This is zero firing! Pull and mark after each shot!"

A few seconds later there was a sharp smack as the first bullet hit the target above them. Carleton jumped to pull the target down, and the conversation was over.

By the end of the week the treatment was getting Andy. Carleton had warmed up enough to heckle him occasionally, even when he was coaching Andy's firing.

There was a second, after he had fired from the kneeling position at two hundred yards, when Andy thought the kid was relaxing. Someone farther up the firing line had evidently been making a miserable score, for the loudspeaker blared at him, "Point Sixteen! Quit wasting the taxpayers' money! Fix bayonets and *charge!*" Carleton, convulsed with laughter, pounded Andy on the back and shoulders. But then he remembered himself again and was as grim as ever.

Andy's score was 235—an expert's score; except for the heckling, it might have been even higher.

Carleton showed himself not at all impressed. "I'll bet that's just average shooting," he said, "for some of you millionaire sportsmen."

Andy jerked himself around, ready to lower the boom at last. In his anger, he forgot the position of his rifle, which pointed straight up.

"Point Thirty-one!" said the loudspeaker. "Your weapon is supposed to be pointed down-range! On your feet! Weapon above your head! Double-time to the end of the point and back!"

❖

On Friday night they came in off the ranges. Tired as he was, Andy spent much time and effort on a letter to his mother. While he had no wish to see her yet, all his anger at her had worn away, and he was anxious to erase as best he could the harshness of whatever he had said to her.

Her intentions, he reflected, had been good by her standards. As for her methods, they were methods he had often used himself.

"I know I was snappish and I wish I hadn't been," he said in his letter. "Blame it on this Army stuff which is all new and confusing and a real workout day in and day out. Another four weeks and the worst part of it will be over, so bear this in mind and bear with me. Be a good girl and I will send you a scenic panorama of Beautiful La Salada in genuine burnt leather."

He took the letter to the orderly room and dropped it through the slot in the door of Pfc Polier's little cubicle. Feeling much better, he was on his way back to his barracks when he saw Hanna rounding the corner of the mess hall.

"Good evening," Andy said a bit tentatively.

"Good evening, Mr. Sheaffer," said the first sergeant. "Didn't expect to see you around here on a weekend. Everything all right? Everything comfortable?"

"Sure," said Andy, holding himself in. "Why not?"

"If they don't treat you just right," said Hanna, "you come and tell me. Because we aim to please."

He continued on his way, whistling merrily, and Andy discovered that he did not feel better after all.

❖

Dear Friend [the form letter had said], you are cordially invited to attend the Open House ceremony in this Company on Saturday . . . from eight until one o'clock.

During the morning the members of this Company will demonstrate their acquired skill in various military drills and will be free to escort their guests on a tour of the Company Area. A weapons display will feature the Infantry weapons fired by your Sponsor during basic training.

Lunch will be served in the Company Mess Hall from twelve until one o'clock. Following the meal all personnel will be issued off-post passes and will be excused until eleven o'clock Sunday night. . . .

A detailed map has been provided on the reverse side of this letter to aid in guiding you to the Company Area. In case of doubt, please feel free to request information from the Military Police guard at the gate.

❖

Fox Company's gaunt and awkward military aspect strained hard to be civilian. Sergeant Stormcloud—"Little Beaver"— had assumed command of the decorations committee, and under his fretful supervision—for he was a marvelously conscientious little man—the members of the company had labored hard to transform the severely tidy into the hospitably pretty.

The cords that roped off and protected the center area of every squad room had been removed at five minutes before eight. The big sign on the front of the orderly room now read INFORMATION CENTER, and a strip of cardboard covered the part that said "Knock and Remove Cap before Entering." The sign-out book had been replaced by a guest roster. Across both ends of the company street, huge banners crackled idly in the breeze.

WELCOME TO OPEN HOUSE
CO. "F"—71st U. S. INFANTRY REGT.

For the occasion, the company commander had pushed his helmet liner up above his eyebrows and now looked upon the rest of mankind from its own level.

Civilian relatives and friends of the trainees milled about the company street, wandered in and out of the barracks, and gaped at the training weapons on display—mortars, machine guns, a tank that someone had fetched up from somewhere—weapons as unfamiliar to their soldier boys as to themselves.

One anxious mother gazed at a 105-millimeter recoil-less ("reckless") rifle mounted on a jeep. "What's *that?*" she asked.

Her son shrugged. "How would I know?"

Officers of the most exalted ranks—captains, majors, light-colonels, and such—strolled about, straining to look interested and friendly. Mayors of three neighboring towns were there, one of them completely sober. The regimental commander was to lunch in Sergeant Hofeller's gorgeously festooned mess hall, Ulcer Alley, and there was talk that the company area would be graced briefly by the presence of the Twelfth Division commander, Major General Two-Star Hennessey himself.

Maguire was one of the six unattached trainees elected as guides. Wearing an armband and white gloves, he strolled about the area looking gracious and affable and answering any question that came his way.

"Your son, madam? Know him very well. One of the most outstanding young men I've ever had assigned to me. I have my eye on that boy!" Or, "That's a very technical question, sir. If you'll drop in at our Information Center and ask for Sergeant Hanna, H-a-n-n-a, I'm sure he'll be glad to answer it for you. Tell him Colonel Whippet sent you."

Andy, clad in a white jacket, was one of the volunteer waiters in the mess hall. Expecting no visitors, he was happy to find something to do to keep him out of the way. His one civilian encounter in the company street had been uncomfortable. Carleton's mother, looking for her son, had seen his name tag, introduced herself, and begun gushing to him about how much his friendship meant to her Henry. She was quoting

Carleton to that effect when the boy himself came upon the scene. "That's right, Mamma," he had said. "Private Sheaffer is quite a boy."

The luncheon was over. The colonel had made a little speech, and a Mrs. Wilkinson had had a corsage presented to her for being the visitor from the farthest distance, and the photographers had littered the mess hall with flashbulbs, and now the place was quiet again.

Andy was helping to clean up the dining room when the door opened and Little Beaver bore down upon him with his earnest little short-legged stride. "Hey, Shafe!" Stormcloud boomed. "You got your wires crossed somewhere. You weren't expecting company."

"Nope," said Andy.

"You got a visitor. Car up at the end of the street."

Andy was puzzled. "Look like my parents?" he asked.

Stormcloud rolled his eyes. "She don't look like no parent to me. She looks real extracurricular to me."

"Blond?"

"Kind of browny," said the sergeant. "One of those bangtail haircuts. Well, don't just stand there, boy!"

❖

The car, parked on the shoulder across the road, was his own little MG. Susan sat behind the wheel, trying to look very cheerful and casual.

For almost three months he had trained himself not to think of her, not to miss her, and now, suddenly, all of it came surging back. Strangely, now that she was here, she seemed farther away than ever. Crisp and lovely and smiling; familiar, and still somehow a stranger.

"Hi, Andy," she said. The tone of her voice was shaky after all, and the greeting was altogether inappropriate.

"Sweetie!" he said. "What are you doing here?"

She waved her hand, but whatever the gesture was meant to be, it did not quite achieve it. "I was coming up to San Fidel," she said, "and your father asked me to drive the Bug up for you. And so."

"San Fidel?" said Andy.

"That's where my grandmother lives."

"Oh," said Andy.

He looked at her, wondering what to say next. If he could think of just the right thing, perhaps it could pull everything back together. He could not get it, though. He could not think of anything at all.

"You don't have to stand there in the road, do you?" said Susan. She maneuvered her trim legs around the brake lever and hoisted herself across to the other side, leaving room for him at the wheel. He paused, got into the car, sat hesitantly for several seconds, and took both her hands. It was almost a simple nervous gesture, but it felt good.

"I can't—" He stopped and started over again. "It's just that it's just such a *surprise*."

"You look just wonderful," said Susan. "You've had a haircut."

"Three," said Andy.

"Well, it's very becoming. What's the white jacket for?"

"I wasn't expecting anybody," he said, looking at the jacket as if it were the first time he had seen it, "so I volunteered to be one of the waiters."

"You're very versatile," said Susan.

"They teach us lots of things," said Andy.

"I think you look just wonderful," said Susan.

"You look wonderful too," said Andy. "How've you been? And what have you been doing?"

"Oh, nothing much, I guess. Just sort of knocking around with my grandmother. She's exhausting, really."

"Hmmm," said Andy, looking very sober and thoughtful.

"I suppose you've been quite busy," said Susan.

"Well, yes," said Andy. "You know how it is."

"I can imagine," said Susan.

Their position—they were half-turned toward each other in the cramped little car—was not particularly comfortable. The four hands held on to one another, none of them quite knowing how to comport themselves. The conversation, feeble from birth, died completely while the two of them looked each other over.

"Would you like to see the company area?" he asked at long last. "I think I could wrangle some lunch too."

"I'd love to see the company area," she said with something like relief. "I'm not very hungry, though."

They strolled about the almost empty area. She wanted to see his very own rifle, and the bunk where he slept, and he even opened his wall locker for her. "I'm just overcome," she said. "It's so neat! It isn't like you!"

This was the nearest they had come to any identity with their old selves, and he was grateful and comforted. "Yeah," he said. "They're teaching me that the hard way."

"Do you like all this?" she asked as they headed back toward the car. "What I mean, are you adjusting to it?"

"I don't particularly like it," he said. "But what the hell. I've just about determined to do it. If this is it, I guess I'll take the bounce."

"I've missed you," she said.

"I've missed *you*," said Andy. "It's an awfully long time."

"We'll have to make up for it," she said. "Are you going to be able to drive me to San Fidel?"

"I wish I could," said Andy, "but I'm on details for now. There's nobody here but us volunteers."

"I like volunteers."

"I'll have to get a cab for you."

"If you can get out tomorrow, and over to San Fi, I'll make you a real civilian dinner."

"I can't," he said. "I'm stuck for the whole weekend."

"All right," said Susan. "Some other time." She sounded strangely, pathetically chin-uppish.

"Oh no, sweetie," said Andy. "Not like that. Let's say next weekend."

"Sure," said Susan. "Now call me a taxi."

Here, said Andy, we've found the magic word. "All right," he said. "You're a taxi."

She looked at him, first curiously, then happily, and both of them bellowed with laughter and relief. A connection had been made.

❖

There were three grenade courses. In the first of them the routine consisted of little more than lying there in the dirt and throwing the toy pineapples where the man told you to. The second was not really anything, either. You listened to the instructor's shopworn spiel through the squawk-box, and watched the earnest pantomime of the demonstrator on the platform, and then you crawled off through a lot of boondock, hollering at the top of your voice in the good old Army way.

("Enthusiasm!" said Maguire, who was already displeased because he had planned to get out of that day's problem and had failed shamefully. "If they want to hear enthusiasm from me, all they have to do is hand me a discharge.")

The third course was a strangely sinister-looking place called the Grenade Pit. Its small area was enclosed on two sides by great concrete walls. On the near wall, protected somewhat from the enclosure, a young lieutenant stood on a low observation platform. His face was hard and capable, his voice crisp and serious.

"Good morning, men," he said, and the first bite of his voice had them all alert. "I'm Lieutenant Ruge, Weapons Committee, Division Faculty." He paused. "For the next few minutes, you men will be throwing live grenades."

Andy looked at Carleton. Carleton shivered.

"The same type of grenades they use in combat," said the lieutenant. "One fragmentation, one concussion. I suggest while you're here you stay awake, listen to me, think—and we'll have no sweat.

"Now, specifically, here's what happens. The first rank, you're the first order. The second rank, you're the second order."

Andy, without knowing why, wished he could at least have been spared being in the first rank.

"After this orientation, first rank, you will proceed to the ammo point. At the ammo point you will pick up one brown fragmentation grenade and one black concussion grenade. You will go around the corner into your pits.

"As soon as you hit the pits, without a command from anyone, put your weapon down on the right—operating handle up, barrel facing up the hill. Set the grenades down by your left shoulder. Get down into a prone position and follow all commands from me. I will be in the tower."

"I wish," said Carleton, "that I was in the tower."

"Now, get this!" shouted the lieutenant. "Do not touch your grenades! Do not move around! Do not touch a thing until I tell you to do so! I will be in the tower! You will follow all commands from me! I will go through it step by step, and when you are throwing grenades there will be a cadreman in the pit to assist you.

"Second order, you will do an about-face. On both sides of the main tower you will find a periscope. You will look through the periscope, listen to what I have to say—and you watch while the first twelve men fire. After they fire, you will fire."

Andy did some quick figuring. He was not only in the first

order; he was going to be one of the first twelve men. On his
left was Carleton; on his right, one of the Mexican kids. Somewhere behind him, safe in the second order, was the fortunate
Maguire. Maguire was sure to do a quick shuffle, be behind the
periscopes for both phases of the function.

"Once again," said the lieutenant, "let me emphasize the
seriousness of these grenades!"

Please don't, said Andy. It's been emphasized more than
enough already.

"Stay awake—think—follow me—and we'll have no trouble!
First order! Now, *if the grenade should drop*, the first thing you
will do, you will sound off, loud and clear, 'Live grenade!' "

Andy could hear Henry Carleton whispering to the man beyond him, "If he doesn't stop talking about it, I'm not going
to do it. I'm just yellow."

"You will pick the grenade up, throw it out of the pit, and
land in a prone position!"

Fact is bad enough, said Andy. Spare us the fantasy.

"If you cannot throw it out of the pit," the instructor continued relentlessly, "on three sides of the pit there is a grenade
sump! Push or roll that grenade into the grenade sump! Land
outside the pit in a prone position!

"First order, *move out!*"

The first order moved out to the ammunition point. Andy
picked up his two grenades and followed the line into the pits.
The apples felt strangely heavy in his hands, and when he
looked at them one was as ugly and lethal-looking as the other.

Hanson give him a little slap on the shoulder, and he took
his position in Pit 4. He laid his rifle down on one side and
the grenades on the other and took another look at Hanson
before dropping to the prone. The acting sergeant's face was
as placid as ever. "Remain flexible," he said to Andy. "This has
been done before."

"Above your head," said the loudspeaker, "you will see a

red circle. Within that red circle there is a white number. Raise your head and take a look at that number. Do not move, do not touch your grenades, until I call your number."

Andy raised his head. Number Four.

"One, three, five, seven, niner, and eleven!" said the lieutenant. "Secure one black concussion grenade! Pick it up in your left hand, place it in your right! Your right thumb is over that safety lever! *On your feet!*"

To his left, in Pit 3, Carleton arose, looking gray. On his right, in 5, Hernandez stood up. Hernandez *always* looked frightened.

"Face the cadremen," said the loudspeaker, "and get into a good pull-pin position! The grenade is vertical, right in front of the chin. Index finger in the pull ring, elbows up, forearm parallel to the ground. Pit Seven, get your elbows up! Pit Nine looks good!"

There was a long, taut, expectant moment of silence, and then the loudspeaker resumed, very slowly. "With a twisting, pulling mo-shahn . . ."

And then, loud and sharp and not nearly so assured: *"Pit Five! What the hell are you doing?"*

Pit 5, Andy suddenly realized, was the one next door. He twisted about and looked off to his right. Above the parapet he could see Hernandez, his face full of revulsion and panic, wrestling prematurely with the safety pin of his grenade. If there was any conscious thought in Hernandez' mind, it could be only the thought of throwing the fearful bomb as far as he could, as quickly as he could.

"Cadreman in Pit Five! Watch your man!"

Hanson was watching, in horrified fascination. As he watched, Hernandez managed to extricate the pin with a jerk so violent that the grenade flew out of his hand and over his shoulder. It rolled a few inches on the dirt, and came to a stop halfway between Hernandez' pit and Andy's.

"Live grenade!"

There was a violent montage of sights and sounds and the sense of time suspended. There were sharp, confused commands from the tower, and no move to obey them. From the far end of the line, someone—it looked like the company commander— approached at a dead run. Hernandez was frozen. So was Hanson.

From somewhere earlier in the day, Andy remembered the words "four seconds." How long is four seconds, he wondered, and how does one count them? He was conscious that he himself was moving, in a fantastic sort of slow motion, and he vaguely wondered where and why. His leg shot out behind him in the same dreamlike slowness, and his foot wafted out, and his instep slapped the grim black can. With the same elaborate slowness, the grenade rolled to the edge of the sump, hung there, and dropped out of sight.

He closed his eyes for a second, then opened them again when he felt the annoying sensation of something wet being held against his nose. Almost touching his own face, it seemed, was the anxious, motherly face of little Sergeant Stormcloud, and the wet thing was a bloody handkerchief.

"Get away," said Andy. "What the hell are you doing?"

"Take it easy," said the Field First. "Just a little nose-bleed."

There was a tremendous ringing in Andy's head. He looked painfully about, and found that he was propped against a tree on a hillside. "What happened?" he demanded.

"Boy, you're built solid," Stormcloud said shakily. "That concrete sump has got a crack in it three inches wide."

Andy pushed at the little Comanche and tried to raise himself.

"Rest easy, soldier," said Stormcloud. "You don't move until the medics say you can."

❖

The first-soldier of Fox Company stuck his lean and grizzled head into the company commander's office as if he were not sure that anyone lived there. The company commander sat at his desk, his expression that of a steer that has been pole-axed not quite effectively enough. At the other desk, Lieutenant Taylor sat wishing there was something he could do.

"It's certainly peaceful in here for a change," said Sergeant Hanna. "No music. You kids' phonograph gone bust?"

"Nothing is busted," said the company commander, "except the first man who reaches to turn the damned thing on."

"How're you feeling by now?" asked the first sergeant.

"I feel," said Lieutenant Jennison, "like somebody's spent the day beating on my helmet with a stick. With me inside. I find the tiniest little noise excrucitating."

"You better go home and sack in," said Hanna.

"Well," said the lieutenant, "I want to look at those people again."

"They're all right," said Hanna. "No casualties. I was just down to the Third Platoon."

"And?" said Jennison.

"Well," said Hanna, "I'm not going to say it's our most efficient fighting arm right now. It's the sorriest damned sight I ever saw. Half the troops are flaked out, and the other half are gassing their heads off in the latrine."

"How's Golden Boy?"

"He'll be all right," said the First. "He and the others close by won't have any duty tomorrow, and that's meat and drink for that boy."

"Stop picking on him," said Lieutenant Taylor. "He's earned his day off."

"Yes," said Lieutenant Jennison. "I'm real fond of that boy this evening."

"All right," Hanna said agreeably. "Just don't go making any speeches to him, or giving him a direct commission in the field. Okay?"

"He did you a favor," said Taylor. "You wouldn't want to have to break in a new commanding officer."

"Lord, no," said Hanna. "I've barely got this one trained. I just don't want the boy thinking he's done something heroic, like they seem to think down in the platoon."

"Hanna," said the company commander, "you're complacient and uncivil. It might not have been a heroic deed, but, by grannies, it was a very nice gesture!"

nine

"IT'S A BLONDE this time," said Stormcloud. "And she's parked down at *that* end of the street."

Andy took a further look at him, to make sure that he was not kidding, and then managed to say thanks. Little Beaver stood there expectantly. "Just waiting further instructions," he said. "Because if you don't want her, I'm not proud."

"I'll manage it," said Andy. "I'll manage it." He strode down the company street, and there she was, parked across the end of it. The view was partially blocked by the figure of Private Ransom Maguire, who was having trouble convincing himself that his services were not required.

"I'll just wait," Maguire was saying to Maggi. "I don't like to see young girls—dazzling young girls—left unprotected in the midst of a pack of howling wolves. These soldiers are half-savage. The sight of you could completely unglue them. Then

too, your young man might be out in the boondocks somewhere."

"You're thoughtful and gallant," said Maggi. "And absolutely
off base. Here is the young man now."

"Maggi!" said Andy. "What are you doing out *here*?"

"Just passing by," she said, "and saw your light."

Andy looked at Maguire. Maguire looked at Andy. "Well?"
said Maguire rather severely.

"Miss Van Kleef," said Andy, "Private Maguire."

"Pleasure," said Maguire, "is no word for it."

"Enchanted," said Maggi.

"Private Maguire," said Andy, "hail and farewell."

Maguire sighed deeply. "Miss Van Kleef," he said, "I'm
sure that fate will bring us together again."

"Undoubtedly," said Maggi with a trace of what might very
well have been resignation.

"Are you all right?" she said to Andy when they were at last
relatively alone. "I read about the grenade in the newspaper.
I was awfully worried about you."

"Sound as a dollar," said Andy. "Sounder, really."

"Can we go anywhere?" said Maggi.

"Sure," he said. "Service club."

He got in beside her, and they drove away and found a
fairly quiet corner in the club cafeteria.

"You look a little different," she said, studying his face with
an almost maternal closeness. "Shell shock?"

He laughed. "That's silly. I'm all right."

"That weird weekend," she said, "I was really worried about
you. You looked like a real borderline. I was afraid you were
going to do something."

"You should have seen me the day after," said Andy, "when
the first sergeant finished with me. That boy dug three feet
deep to find me a lower spot on the totem."

She laid her hand briefly on his and gave him a couple of

pats. "You'd never know it now," she said. "That must have been a real therapeutic little hand grenade."

Andy laughed. "Let's say it shook me up a little. I'm re-settling real cool."

"For instance," said Maggi.

"Well," said Andy, "the dust cleared, and I looked around, and for the first time I was able to figure out who I was and what I was doing. I may not be the model soldier, but at least I've got damned good reflexes."

"Is that all?" said Maggi, twinkling at him.

"When you come right down to it, I think it is."

"Andy," she said, "do you feel like talking?"

"Sure," he said. "Talk."

"I don't know why, but I got the feeling that you were sounding different *before* this grenade bit. On the phone you sounded different. What happened? Mail from home?"

"Sort of," he said.

"The girl?"

"She's here in the neighborhood now."

"How do you feel?"

"I don't know. I'm trying to figure it out."

She took a deep, open-mouthed breath before going on. "I like you, Andy Sheaffer," she said. "Do me a favor. See this girl a lot."

"Why?"

"You'll either get her out of your system or back in, and either way is good for you. Good for me too. We're both too nice to go rebounding on each other."

He thought it over for a long time, and then he looked up at her face again. "Have you ever been kissed," he said, "in a service-club cafeteria?"

"No," she said, "but I'll try anything once."

❖

From the notebooks of Private Maguire:

211. He has two and I have none. The one who was here for Open House looks young and wholesome and just the type for A. J. Sheaffer. I must simplify this boys life for him, even at grt personal sacrifice. O Maguire, you fool, you fool, you fool. Here we go again.

212. C Rations served in mess hall twice a week, beans and weenies. Always prepared as a regular meal, so whats the point. Question: who gets the cigs that come in C Rations. Good thing for these noncoms they have a strong union.

213. Talked to a soldier in Svc Club Cafeteria today, he has run into the wierdest deal of all. Was put on a Wild Life Detail, trapping squirrels and collecting fleas off them. Question: What does the Army need with fleas. Army has no shortage of flies on it.

214. Chaplain in this area has friendly manner but is actually R.A. all the way. Says he isn't here to coddle the troops. Tells a man you can train in the company like a soldier or in the stockade like a prisoner. Says train with a gun in yr hand or a gun in yr back, and the choice is yr own. What kind of talk is this from a Chaplain? The I.G. should hear about it.

215. The perfect deal, startling in its simplicity. Go to supply room, draw one (1) hammer and one (1) ladder. Proceed with these to end of co. street. Supply room will figure your working for orderly room, and vice versa. Place hammer and ladder under edge of day room and take off for Svc Club or wherever.

❖

After the long weeks Andy had spent in combat boots, the light, low-cut Italian shoes felt like bedroom slippers. There was an almost silky luxuriousness in the texture of what had once been an ordinary gingham shirt. And the tweed sports jacket seemed illicitly loose and easygoing.

By George, he said as he reviewed himself in the tall mirror beside the orderly-room door, these civilians know how to make clothes!

He had forgotten, too, the joyful feel of the little MG. At first it was somewhat confused and reluctant, because it had been sitting there idle in the post parking lot for almost two weeks, but it came to with a little cranking, and, once out upon the highway, it roared and bounced and responded joyfully to his touch.

He was feeling remarkably good himself by the time he found the sprawling old Daniel house in San Fidel.

The door was opened by a rather frightening little old lady with extremely shrewd but not unfriendly eyes and a booming and positive voice. She catalogued his face, studied his clothing as if it were not exactly what she had ordered, and finally thrust a bony little hand at him. "You're Sheaffer," she said, and it sounded as if it were a name she was assigning to him.

"Yes, ma'am," said Andy, a little awed by her.

"Come in, Sheaffer!" she said. "Find a chair; that's a good one over there! I'm old Mrs. Daniel. Susan will be down sooner or later."

"Thank you," said Andy.

"Just like the Army," said Mrs. Daniel. "Hurry up and wait."

"Yes, ma'am," said Andy. The living room was large and pleasant, and it had evidently spent a lifetime accumulating the lush clutter of memorabilia it contained. Above an ancient chest against the far wall, he noticed with a start, hung the large oil portrait of an elderly man with an ironic twinkle and the uniform of a major general.

"That's George," said Mrs. Daniel. "He won't bite. Looks mean as hell, doesn't he?"

"A little," said Andy.

"Most harmless general officer the Army ever produced," said Mrs. Daniel. "Cast-iron outside, mushy underneath. We liked him, though."

In his present situation Andy was not quite able to think of any general as harmless, but he studied the painting with interest. At the very least, it explained a number of things about Little Sobersides. He knew that there was a nasty little Army taint somewhere in the pedigree, but he had never suspected that it was this deep. He had never imagined that there was insanity in the family.

Mrs. Daniel's voice broke in upon him. "You beginning to like the Army? Think you might make a career of it?"

"No, ma'am," said Andy. "It just doesn't hit me that way."

"That's good," she said. "Good, solid head on your shoulders. I wasn't sure. Susan says you've been playing around with live hand grenades."

"Yes, ma'am."

"Good thing to stay away from. You're all right now, aren't you? No lasting damage?"

He had no time to answer. Susan charged into the room, gave him a light kiss and a lingering inspection, and dismissed her grandmother from the scene. "Away with you," she said. "Go play poker with your cronies."

"All right," said Mrs. Daniel. "I will. And, Susan, play this young man right. This one I like."

"Why?" said Susan.

"Just like him. There's something about him," said her grandmother. "I like a boy who's able to carry on an intelligent conversation."

❖

Susan closed the door behind the old lady, came back to Andy's chair, and sat upon the arm of it. She studied his face for a very long time, probing deep into his eyes. He was at a loss for something to say, and then he realized that there was nothing he should say. When she bent to kiss him, he pulled her down into his lap and cradled her like a small child.

"It feels like old times," he said.

"I wish it were," said Susan. "I've been so *lonely*."

"There's been a lot of that going around," said Andy.

"If I were you," said Susan, "I wouldn't even talk to me."

"If you were me"—he laughed—"who'd be you?"

"Don't be so elderly and wise," she said. "It's not becoming to you. You're the last person on earth to be elderly and wise."

"That's what I figured all along," said Andy. "I've been trying to overcome it—with the cooperation of our armed services."

"You remember what I said to you that horrible Sunday?"

"Nope."

"You do too. I told you you were childish and you'd never grow up. I've been figuring it out, Andy. I'm the childish one."

"That'll be the day," said Andy.

"Except," she said, "I'm not childish in the nice, wonderful way you are."

"Well, I can tell you," said Andy, "that don't come easy."

"But the worst—the very worst—was all that screeching about your being fun-crazy. You know something?"

"Very little."

"I haven't had any fun at all since that awful Sunday. Not one damned bit. All you have to do is ask for adulthood, and it comes pouring in on you."

Andy compassionately patted her flank. "You don't even have to ask for it."

"Do you still feel fun-loving?"

"I haven't aged that much." He laughed. "There's still something smoldering in the ashes."

"How do you feel now?"

"Comfortable," said Andy. "Serene. And just the teeniest bit lecherous."

"I'm glad," said Susan.

"But above all," said Andy, "fun-loving." The hand that had been patting moved up to her beltline, carrying her sweater with it, and found a grip upon the warm, familiar waist beneath.

Susan stirred languidly. "You may stroke," she said, "but no tickling!"

"Fool!" said Andy. "You are in my power."

❖

Mad Margaret opened her front door and looked out. "Oh," she said. "I was hoping it was only a bill collector."

"Miss Van Kleef," said Maguire. "Perhaps you do not remember me. I am Ransom Maguire. Private Ransom Maguire, so called. The good gray friend of Private A. J. Sheaffer."

"My heartiest congratulations," said Maggi.

"I fell by," said Maguire, "on a very reluctant mission. It is my painful duty to inform you that Private A. J. Sheaffer, due to the vicissitudes of life and the fortunes of war, will be unable to show."

"So?" said Maggi.

"It has been deemed essential to the military effort that Private Sheaffer remain at his battle station this weekend, keeping always on the alert and observing everything that takes place within sight or hearing."

"Isn't that a shame!" said Maggi.

"Private Sheaffer has asked me, as his oldest and dearest friend, to apprize you of the situation. To tender his profound regrets. To solace you in this moment of bereavement. May I come in?"

"Private Ransom Maguire," said Miss Van Kleef, "no one

could ever accuse you of having one honest bone in your body."

"I'm afraid I don't grasp your meaning," said Maguire.

"My meaning is this," said Maggi. "You can stop giving me the big hypo—because, Jack, you have missed the vein."

"Madam?" said Maguire.

"Or," she said, "if I must hyphenate the words for you, you can lay off the heavy lard. I didn't just get into town on a load of peaches."

"I'm afraid you do me wrong," said Maguire.

"Let me clue you, Private Maguire," said Maggi. "I am well aware that Private Sheaffer will not be here today. I was told this by Private Sheaffer himself. Private Sheaffer is not on weekend duty of any savor or description. He has a date. This was well understood by all parties concerned. Therefore! What are *you* doing around, with your hand full of sweetheart roses and a disarming little Kingfish grin on your face?"

The grin on Maguire's face unfolded itself, revealing clear-eyed and impenitent knavery. "You overwhelm me," he said. "If you ever go into police work, God help all honest thieves."

"You *are* ashamed of yourself, aren't you?" said Maggi. "Trying to undercut your best friend?"

There was a repressed but unmistakable crinkling at the corners of her large, clear eyes, and Maguire was not the type to overlook it.

"I hate myself for it," said Maguire, "but I'm hopeless. I'm drawn to you, Miss Van Kleef—irresistibly drawn. The first look at your dear, sweet, extracurricular face, and I was down for the count of ten."

"Oh, brother!" said Maggi.

"The truth is," he said, "love hits hard at my time of life."

She threw her head back and loosed her heartiest laughter. "Maguire," she said, "shame is not in you! How anybody can stand on a girl's front porch, with his foot in the door, in the middle of a Saturday afternoon, and shuck that horrible corn—"

"If you were a kindly woman," said Maguire, "I would not be standing on a front porch at all. I would be sitting inside, with a cold beer in my hand, and you would be listening with sympathetic interest to my sad story."

"You are utterly *impossible!*" she said with mounting wonder. "All right. Come in. You can have one beer—one, mind you— while I'm calling for the wagon."

❖

"Now look," said Carleton. "This guard mount tomorrow, they're playing with the blue chips. If you want to come home with your skin on, you better not potsky around with it."

"Okay," said Andy, laughing wearily. "How many briefings you going to give me?"

"I'm not harassing," said Carleton. "I just want to make sure you're checked out on it. You better let me give that rifle of yours the double-C."

Andy twisted on his bunk, picked up the rifle, and handed it to his earnest young friend. "Look it over," he said, "but don't breathe on it."

Carleton examined the weapon inside and out, and, finding nothing amiss, began examining it all over again. When he lifted one foot and propped it on the other knee, Andy was almost blinded by the glare.

"Mother, Mother, Mother!" he said. "What have you got on those boats? Oil of chromium?"

"That's just an ordinary job of spit polish," said Carleton. "That's the way yours are supposed to look too."

"Henry," said Andy, "I'm not aiming for perfection. All I want to do is look presentable, not ostentatious!" He looked at Carleton's shoes again, and then at his own. "All right. So be it. You going to show me how?"

"Nothing to it," said Carleton. "You get those boots good

and clean, like it was your rifle. Then you put the polish on, a little at a time—not even as big a space as a penny—and then you work it in with your fingers."

"This is ridiculous," said Andy, but he went to work. He was working it in with his fingers when Maguire got back from the shower. Maguire had been much less garrulous the past few days, as if he were preoccupied. He was not at all bemused now. He looked at Sheaffer, rolled his eyes, and disgustedly threw the wet towel on his bunk. "Absolutely no sense of values!" he said. "I mean it! None!"

"Better get spruced up, Bruce," Andy said good-naturedly. "A sloppy uniform is the sign of a sloppy soldier."

"Oh, get him!" said Maguire. "What's with you, Sheaffer? You blown a fuse or something?" He turned indignantly to Carleton. "You I could understand, because you're essentially stupid."

"Bottom of the class," Carleton said affably.

"Henry, you've seen what I've tried to do for that boy. I do things the hard way. I go out and work my fingers to the bone because I want to get ahead in the Army. I ingratiate myself with the cadre; I let them use my magnificent brain on their damned dull paper work. And why? Just so that a little of their friendship and admiration for me will rub off on my friends."

"Thank you, Father," said Andy. "Peace, it's wonderful."

"If he listened to me, he'd have this whole military routine locked going in. I know the ropes. I learn them the hard way, and I try to pass them on to you. And you simply will not dig what I'm putting down."

"Ain't that a bite?" said Carleton.

"Laugh," said Maguire. "While you're flaked out in your crummy little sack at night, doing nothing but pressing the blanket and collecting bedsores, you know what I'm doing?"

"Yeah," said Carleton. "You're skulking across A-wol Bridge, dodging the searchlights and listening for the bloodhounds. You're dating some beetle in town, that's what."

"O, monstrous lie!" roared Maguire. "I'll tell you what I'm doing! I'm prowling through the orderly room, sitting up with the charge-of-quarters at battalion, bringing coffee to the deadheads at regimental headquarters! Prying, snooping, listening! Learning the ARs. Picking up the schedule ahead of the company commander. Trying to protect you two. Trying to make a home for you in the Army!"

"Oh, the north wind doth blow," said Andy, "and we shall have snow!" He licked one finger, heavily stained with oxblood, and held it up against the imaginary breeze.

"Work on the heels," said Carleton. "Get *them* good and shiny. When they inspect the guard mount, they get real henhouse about it. Talk about picking flyspecks out of the pepper, this is where you see it."

Andy applied himself to the heel of a shoe.

"All right, then," said Maguire. "Knock your brains out on a lot of nothing. What are you going to get out of it? You going to impress the government? They going to give you a seven-year contract with options?"

"Dad," said Andy, "I'm just learning. Who knows? Maybe I'm picking up a useful trade for civilian life."

❖

Hanna looked up, and his frown mellowed a little when he saw that it was Hanson. "What's your problem, old-timer?" he asked the retread.

"Sergeant," said Hanson, "it's been looking to me like you were riding this boy Sheaffer. Is that a fact?"

"You might say that," said Hanna. "Bracing him, like. He seems to me like a light operator."

"Well, I don't know," said Hanson. "I've had my troubles with him. He seems to be making the effort now, though."

"I'm happy to hear that," said the First.

"So I was just thinking, maybe if you let up on him for a while—"

"Sure," said Hanna. "I'll let up on him. The minute he starts showing me something."

Hanson had no chance to say anything further. The voice of Corporal Goldberg, the company clerk, rolled across the orderly room and into the topkick's office. "Sergeant Hanna! It's for you!"

The first sergeant sighed and picked up the phone. "Sergeant Hanna, sir!" he said.

"Well, a good, good day to you, Sergeant Hanna!" said a basso profundo voice at the other end. Hanna winced; it was the voice of the battalion sergeant major, and the sound of it usually meant trouble. He waited for the trouble. "Sergeant McCarthy here!"

"I know who the hell it is," said Hanna. "What is it this time?"

"Just a friendly invitation, sergeant," said the sergeant major. "Some of the older noncoms are holding a clandestyne meeting tonight out behind the Paint Shed. Going to get together and talk old-fashioned Army talk, four-letter words and all."

"Oh, goody," said the first sergeant.

"Sergeant Weithas from the motor pool has volunteered to be the private."

"Now," said Hanna, "what did you *really* call me about?"

"Called to give you greetings," said the sergeant major, "from the Department of the Army!"

"I knew it," said Hanna. "I could feel it in my bones. Another one of them cute little mandatory levies?"

"They want forty-five squad leaders from the Twelfth Division," said McCarthy. "Division wants five of them to come from the Seventy-First Infantry."

"Don't come to me," said Hanna. "I've been picked clean

already. I mean it, McCarthy. I haven't got 'em. I've got one damned corporal in this whole unit, and he's the Training NCO."

"All right, then," said the sergeant major. "Find us an old sergeant somewhere."

"McCarthy," said Hanna, "don't do it to me."

"As broodmaster of Company F," said McCarthy, "you will submit, by oh-nine-hundred hours tomorrow, the name of one cadreman with the MOS of one-one-one-point-six-oh. And that's all she wrote."

"McCarthy! On bended knee!"

"It so states," said the sergeant major, "that a suitable replacement will be forthcoming in the very near future."

"Yeah," said Hanna. "Sure. Will he be coming before—or after—the replacement for the last one you shanghaied out of my company?"

"Why do you always take it so hard?" said McCarthy.

"Sergeant," said Hanna, "it's battle rattle. I can't find cadremen as fast as you take them away. What does the Army do with all those noncoms they steal? There's not that many understrengthed bases out in the desert. There's not that many vacancies overseas. There's no sane reason at all."

There was an eloquent pause at the other end of the line. "I'm looking for a handkerchief," said the sergeant major. "Never have I heard a story that touched me so deeply. There's nothing much I can say, except—"

"Except what?"

"—except that by oh-nine-hundred tomorrow I want one cadreman over here with the Fox Company brand on him."

"All right then, sergeant," said Hanna. "If you can guarantee it's for overseas duty, I'll come over myself."

"Wouldn't you just love that!" said McCarthy. "You lily-livered slacker!" And that ended the conversation.

Hanna laid down the phone and gazed off, completely through

the calendar picture of Marilyn Monroe on the far wall, and into that distant area where dwell the minds of first sergeants.

"Kynch is in your platoon, isn't he?"

"Sure," said Hanson. "Squad leader."

"Could he handle a platoon?"

"He can if I can," said Hanson.

"Anybody to take over his squad?"

"Sure," said Hanson. "You could give it to Carleton. He's a fast-learning little scout."

"I could, at that," said Hanna. "Goldberg! Where are all our lieutenants?"

"I don't know, Sergeant. I never know."

"Gawd," said Hanna. "If the Army ever gets to the place where corporals come as cheap as lieutenants! Where's Stormcloud?"

"He took off half an hour ago with the guard mount. He's sergeant of the guard."

Hanna drummed his fingers irritably on the desk top. He was gazing off through Miss Monroe again when footsteps came up the front stairs. There was a knock, and a wait, and then Private Sheaffer entered, carrying his helmet before him.

"That's all I need!" roared Hanna. "You're supposed to be on guard duty! What the hell are you doing back here? Forget your Superman badge or something?"

Andy came all the way to the office door and paused in the doorway, looking sheepish. Hanna looked at Hanson. Hanson looked at Hanna.

"I was thinking the same thing," said Hanson. "It's possible, but I don't believe it."

"All right, let's have it," said Hanna.

"Somebody seems to have goofed, Sergeant," said Andy. "I'm not walking guard tonight. I've been chosen colonel's orderly for tomorrow."

"You?" said the first sergeant. "*You* are the sharpest-looking private in the regimental guard mount?"

"Yes, sir," said Andy. "They looked me over, and they asked me some General Orders, and chose me the Queen of the May."

Hanna looked at Hanson again. "It shows you," he said, "what Fox Company's coming to if this is the best we can do."

Hanson looked pleased. "It sure does," he said. "Well, Sergeant Hanna, there goes another three-day pass."

ten

THE OFFICE of the regimental commander, a place where Andrew J. Sheaffer had never expected nor aspired to be, was a large room that ran the whole breadth of the second floor of regimental headquarters. The small amount of space in it not filled by the overwhelming presence of the colonel himself was jammed full of flags and banners and trophies and curios. It was not so much an office, Andy decided, as it was a den. It was a rather gaudy den at that.

Andy himself, for that matter, looked somewhat gaudy too. He wore dazzling white leggings, white gloves, and a white helmet liner with a large insignia on it.

The regimental commander suddenly took Andy's hand and propelled him half a step backward so that he would not obscure the regimental banner in the background between them. The colonel held the grip, firm and fervent, and looked into Andy's eyes with almost embarrassing sincerity.

My Lord, said Andy. Six weeks a draftee, and I'm holding hands with a colonel.

Off to his right a flashbulb briefly exploded its light. The colonel's handclasp did not falter, nor did his eyes. Another flashbulb went off. "Well, that's it," said Colonel Whippet, to whom this was a daily occurrence. "You'd better go out there and make sure they've got your home address."

Andy saluted, did a spectacular about-face, and fled into the outer office. "What's all this for?" he asked the sergeant outside.

"They send your picture to your home-town paper," said the sergeant, "with a copy of the letter of commendation."

"I'm all choked up," said Andy.

There was a seismic tremor behind him, and the colonel came whipping out of his office. "If anybody comes looking for me," he said to the sergeant, "I'm out prowling. Let's go!"

Andy tagged along behind him: one step to the left and one to the rear. He followed him, at a gallop, up a street and in and out of two or three battalion headquarters.

Out among the companies, the colonel slowed down a little. Then he stopped altogether to watch a physical-training class far off across the drill field. "You're in the sixth week of basic, is that right?" he said to Andy. "How do you feel?"

"Good, sir."

"Complacent?" said the colonel. "Or just adjusted?"

"Just better, sir," said Andy. "It was pretty jumpy the first few weeks."

"It's not as jumpy as it should be," said the colonel. "You think you're going to make it, though, is that it?"

"Well, sir," said Andy, "there's less than two weeks to go— in basic, that is."

"You like your company?"

"Yes, sir."

"You should. It's a damned good one. How's the food?"

"Fine, sir."

"Don't give me polite answers," said the colonel. "I'm not just killing time this way."

"No, sir," said Andy.

"Down in your company, what's their nickname for me?"

"Old Gung Ho, sir," said Andy, enjoying the opportunity, but remembering not to show it. The colonel seemed to find satisfaction in the answer.

"You look like an intelligent enough young man. I like to pick people's brains."

"Yes, sir."

"If you were commanding officer of your company, who's the first man you'd fire?"

"I wouldn't fire anybody, sir," said Andy. "I'd have to look around first."

"All right," said the colonel, "what would you do besides just looking around? Remember, you're the company commander."

"Yes, sir," said Andy. He savored the prospect a long time before he made his answer. "First off, sir, I would call in my first sergeant, and I would talk to him like a father."

"Speak freely," said the colonel. "What would you say to this first sergeant?"

We might as well go for broke, Andy decided. "I would say to him, sir," he said, " 'Sergeant Hanna, you have been riding high in this company, and now it's my turn. As of this date, sergeant, you can lay your heart upon the altar, for your tail is mine.' "

"On a strictly personal basis," said the colonel.

"Yes, sir," said Andy.

"I have my eye on Sergeant Hanna," said the colonel. "He's a damned good first sergeant, and I'm glad to have you bear that opinion out."

❖

The orderly room was alerted, but barely in time. By a stroke of sheer good fortune Sergeant Shehan happened to be standing on the veranda when they turned into the company street.

Sergeant Shehan zipped back inside and sounded the tocsin. "It's the regimental commander!" he shouted. "Waving the bloody shirt!"

Lieutenant Jennison and the first sergeant leaped from their chairs. Stormcloud began fussing furiously with his pale blue neckerchief. Lieutenant Taylor, with an altogether uncharacteristic show of speed, turned off his phonograph and got it out of sight. Within a matter of seconds, it seemed, the two lieutenants were proceeding gravely down the orderly-room steps. They looked solemn, stiff, and military, as if preoccupied with their vast problems of command and administration.

Taylor, seemingly accidentally, espied the colonel, who was almost upon them. " 'Tchun!" said Lieutenant Taylor, softly and with great dignity. Both lieutenants wheeled about, landing at attention—at a Trade School brace, for that matter—and saluted.

"Good afternoon!" said the colonel in the high, clear, earnestly enthusiastic voice prescribed for officers returning salutes. "Jennison, what the hell kind of rout-step outfit are you running around here? A summer camp for little boys?"

"I beg the colonel's pardon?" said the company commander.

"I come through this area slowly," said Colonel Whippet. "On foot. Eagles on my collar as big as sea gulls. Man in a white pot following right along behind me. Everything but a goddamn steam calliope playing 'The Star-Spangled Banner.' And practically nobody salutes. Have we discarded that quaint old custom in Fox Company?"

"No, sir," said Lieutenant Jennison.

"New directive from Washington that I haven't seen yet? Another little by-product of the goddamn Doolittle Board?"

"No, sir. No excuse, sir."

"Jennison, I want to tell you a thing or two," said the colonel, and he did. When he had finished gnawing upon the lieutenant's posterior, a courtesy that Jennison grimly determined to relay down the entire chain of his little command, a chastened group proceeded down the company street. The colonel continued his barking, but it seemed, at least to Lieutenant Taylor, that he was not at all displeased by the aspect of the area.

That is, until they came to the very end of the street.

Coming down the street, from the general direction of the service club, was Fox Company's official photographer, rifle-roster and morning-report consultant, legal-aid adviser and permanent CQ runner, Private Ransom Maguire. In his right hand he carried a hammer, under his left arm a ladder, and in his mouth a large and redolent cigar.

He saw the brass almost as soon as they saw him. He decided not to turn into the company street, but to continue on, as if he belonged to some fortunate unit farther down the road. He might have got away with it too, for none of the present Fox Company personnel had any overwhelming impulse to acknowledge him at the moment. But the colonel could read, as luck would have it, and the legend stenciled on the front of Maguire's helmet liner said "F-71."

Even then it might not have been seen, except that Maguire pointed it directly at them. He did not slacken his pace, but he tucked the hammer into his left armpit, hurled the group a magnificent salute and a dazzling smile, and sounded off. "Good afternoon! Isn't this a glorious day!"

"Soldier," said the colonel. Maguire screeched to a halt. "Front and center," said the colonel.

"Yes, sir," said Maguire, saluting again.

"You don't salute with a cigar butt in your mouth," said the colonel.

"No, sir," said Maguire.

"How many times have you been up and down this road with that ladder and that hammer?"

"I couldn't say, sir."

"I've seen you on four different occasions," said the colonel, "loping between here and the service-club area. What have you been doing up there?"

Maguire looked at the colonel, then at the lieutenants, and then at his onetime friend and compeer in the white pot. He decided to throw himself on the mercy of the court. "Bugging out, sir."

"I thought as much," said the colonel, obviously a little shaken to find the rug pulled from under him. "There couldn't be that many loose nails in the whole area." He turned to the company commander. "You'll see that this man catches up on his back work?"

"Yes, sir," Jennison said stoutly. "We have our own special facilities for bug-outs."

"From the looks of your company area," said the colonel, "I'd say you damned well needed them."

"Yes, sir," said the lieutenant, rather grimly this time.

"And you," the colonel said to Maguire. "If you need special tools for soldiering on the job, I'd suggest you use small ones. Inconspicuous ones. Ones that can't be seen all the way to regimental headquarters."

He returned their salutes and stalked off up the road, his orderly tagging along behind.

Andy could hear the dialogue behind him, and he knew without looking that the company commander's stony face was no more than a quarter of an inch from the face of Ransom Maguire.

"May I say," the lieutenant was saying, "that you're the sorriest damned excuse for a soldier I ever been saddled with?"

"Yes, sir," said Maguire.

"All right," said Jennison. "You're the sorriest damned excuse for a soldier I ever been saddled with! And I need a volunteer to clean the mess-hall grease trap for seven consectional days! Do I hear a volunteer?"

Sure enough, he did.

❖

In the realistic world of the lower echelons the most fearful military device ever invented is the Trap, Grease, Threaded Style, No. 4510-244-7951. No company mess hall is complete, and no company system of discipline has reached its perfection, without one.

The Army grease trap is an ugly black rectangular box, some two by three by two feet deep, that usually sits out behind the mess hall, close against the wall, near to the kitchen sinks inside. It is an appendage, a spur line, of the drainpipes flowing off from the sinks, and its purpose is, as its nomenclature indicates, the trapping of grease and other unattractive matter washing down from the sinks. It preserves these elements in a hot, soapy, greasy mess that has the slickness and consistency of petroleum jelly.

When the grease trap's heavy lid is unbolted and removed, the whole surrounding area is assaulted by a smell of unparalleled putrefaction. The Army would describe it as a scientifically clean smell, no worse than the kitchen smells of many an ill-run restaurant, but the Army can afford to be detached and impersonal; it is not being run by Privates E-1.

When the nostrils are sufficiently numbed, and the eyes have reluctantly opened themselves again, it can be seen that the interior of the Trap, Grease, is divided into compartments. The compartments seem to be full of a foamy, bubbly grease, a grayish-brown, brackish sort of scum. Actually, they are not. The scum is only superficial; it floats in twenty or twenty-five gallons of water.

Once a day this unpleasant mess is skimmed off into a bucket, which it usually half fills, and is carted away to be disposed of God knows how. This daily ceremonial is not a thing entrusted to just any old member of the lowest enlisted grade. It is, as a matter of course, an honor bestowed upon some private who has come, the day before, to the particular notice and concern of the company commander, the first sergeant, or perhaps even the mess steward himself. A man has to *earn* the grease-trap assignment.

Once a week, as a mark of special distinction, one member of the company is singled out from his fellows and detailed to *clean out* the grease trap. He must dip all the water out of the contraption and then remove from the bottom of the trap the "settlage"—bits of food, bone, and other assorted crud. The compartments of the grease trap are staggered, and there are intricate and relatively inaccessible little nooks in the layout, and the man tidying them finds it almost impossible to finish the job with grease-free elbows.

At least Private Ransom Maguire found it thus. He replaced the heavy lid on its lugs, bolted it down, and then surveyed the settlage on his own uniform and person.

"You finished out there with that grease trap?" the mess steward shouted from the kitchen window.

"I *am* the grease trap," said Maguire. "M-1."

"Well, go clean that gunk off you," said the mess steward, "before you come into my kitchen. When you're all clean, I got more stuff for you to do. I got the cleaning urge on me today, and you and me goan have lots of fun."

Maguire's retort was not quite distinct.

"What did you say, soldier?" said the mess steward.

Maguire remembered, in time, a line from an old movie. "I just said you've got dirty plaster."

❖

Sergeant Hanna looked up at the colonel's recent orderly and then back at the papers on his desk. "Well, Mr. Sheaffer," he said. "Quite an honor, having you drop in."

Andy's smile vanished, and his jaw set again.

"When do you want to pick up your pass?" said Hanna.

"I don't want any pass," said Andy.

"You're not required to want one," said Hanna. "You make colonel's orderly on the guard mount, you've automatically got it coming to you."

"Does it say in the book I have to take it?"

"Nope."

"All right, then. I don't want it."

The first-soldier looked up at him blandly. "Why?"

"Well, sir," said Andy, "I've already had one three-day pass that *wasn't* coming to me, and I figure I owe you three days."

"So?" said Hanna.

"So," said Andy, "I figured that maybe I could give you the three days I've earned. Would that even up the score?"

"No," said the first sergeant, "but it would help. I like to see that kind of thinking from the Home Front."

"Sergeant," said Andy. "One more thing. Have I the first sergeant's permission to say something personal?"

"Go right ahead," said Hanna. "It's not my intention to bottle up your emotions."

"Well, since we're on this snide little basis," said Andy, "I'd like to say this. I think this whole routine of yours is getting pretty goddamn hen-house."

"What routine is that?" said the sergeant.

"This mister business," said Andy. "I work around here, the same as anybody else."

"What would you like to be called?"

"Everybody else," said Andy, "seems to be called soldier."

"You regard yourself as a soldier?" said Hanna.

"Damn it," said Andy, "I'm trying."

"I'll tell you what," said Hanna. "I begin to see a glimmer in you. At least you're cleaning your boots and rifle. Who's the best soldier in your platoon?"

"The new squad leader," said Andy. "Corporal Carleton."

"All right," said Hanna. "You watch Corporal Carleton. When you find yourself working like him and acting like him and thinking like him—when you find yourself interested in doing something with a day instead of just killing it—then you come back here and complain about my attitude. Is that clear?"

"Yes, sir."

"Is that satisfactory?"

"Yes, sir."

"All right, then," said Hanna. "Move out."

❖

Lieutenant Jennison came out of the inner office and stood looking quizzically at his first sergeant.

"I thought you were out," said Hanna. "Goofing off somewhere."

"It's a damned poor first sergeant don't know when the CO is around," said Jennison. "You're getting complacient, or either old. Was that Sheaffer you were reaming?"

"That's him," said the First.

"How come you're still riding him?" said the lieutenant.

"That's my system with that type," said Hanna. "Only way to make soldiers out of them."

"He must hate your living guts," said Jennison.

"I hope so," said Hanna. "That's the best part of the system. The more I tell him he's a double-dyed civilian, the more he's going to try to make me out a liar."

"I don't see what you're making such a to-do about," said Jennison. "He looks all right to me. He's quick and steady, and there's no flyspecks on his training chart that I can see."

"Tell you what, Lieutenant," said the first sergeant. "Let's just say he's making a good start once he gets started."

"When I was taking basic," said Jennison, "if I'd have had you for a first sergeant, I'd have gone over the hill."

"Lieutenant," said Hanna, "if you'd had me for a first sergeant, you'd be a major by now."

eleven

"ALL RIGHT one time!" bellowed Little Beaver. "Let's be getting this mess cleaned up! Let's get these troops out of the hot sun!"

The day's work in the bivouac area was over, and the company commander was impatient to get started for home. The men were scheduled to return to the company area the hard way, walking the eight miles with full pack, and Lieutenant Jennison wanted the trip made in what could be literally described as record time. There was a point he wanted to get across to Dog Company, which, the week before, had tied the old Fort Burnside record for the hike. A keen sense of competition pervaded the entire company, or almost all of it, and the lieutenant himself felt it so strongly that he intended personally to lead the march.

One member of Fox Company who did not fully participate in the group feeling was Private Ransom Maguire. From his lofty level of sophistication, it was immaterial to him what happened to any hiking record on earth. And when the length of the walk was eight miles, and the weight of the pack was seemingly greater than his own, nothing could have been less tempting to him.

"Carleton," he said to the acting corporal, "you're a member of the ruling class. It's up to you to do something. You've got to get me out of this."

"Ransom," said Carleton, "just go on and do it like everybody else."

"I'm not like everybody else," Maguire protested. "You're a young man, Henry, and so are all the others. Even the Old Man is a young man compared to me. At my age, and in my state of health, a thing like this could kill me."

"Ransom," said Carleton, "it's only eight miles. A couple of hours' walking is all. Besides, we're going to do the Song!"

"I have friends among the truckdrivers," said Maguire. "I could ride back with the KPs."

"Nothing doing," said Carleton. "We all walk."

With his own squad leader, his own friend and protégé, turned against him, it was going to be almost impossible to eel out of this. But, one way or another, eel out he would. By now the whole thing was a challenge. He was threshing about for a solution when he happened to look across the field, where the more exalted members of the cadre were gathered about the lieutenants. When he saw the company commander looking at his wristwatch he realized that there was no time left. The march was about to begin.

He dug into his jacket pocket, where he kept his number-two notebook, the personal one, and fished it out. Inside it was his sheaf of "emergency papers": blank passes, signed by Jennison and stolen from the orderly room; light-duty slips from the regimental dispensary, none of which he could use on this occasion; dental appointments—all sorts of forms and blanks, all properly signed and ready to be filled in with the name and date. The only thing that looked at all usable and impressive was a form from the post hospital. He scrawled upon it his name, the date, and a time less than an hour away, and rushed over, panting and frowning, to where the lieutenant stood.

"Sir," he said, "I don't think I can make it in time. Not if I have to walk."

"I'd say, then," said Lieutenant Jennison, "that you sure as hell won't make it. Because when I say walk, everybody walks. What have you got there?" He studied the paper that Maguire handed to him, and then he studied Maguire. A warm smile began to blossom upon his rocky young face. "Well, bully for you, Maguire," he said. "Allow me to be the first."

Maguire looked at him blankly.

"My heartiest facilitations and best wishes," the lieutenant continued. He turned suddenly and shouted to the Field First. "Sergeant Stormcloud! Get this man on the mess truck going in!"

"What's up, Lieutenant?" said Little Beaver.

"We're holding up the nuptuals," said Jennison. "This man has got to get back to regiment for a premarital blood test!"

Maguire was aware that his own mouth was hanging ajar.

"By the way, Maguire," said the lieutenant, "who's the lucky lady?"

"I don't think you know her, sir," said Maguire. "She's a civilian."

"What's her name?"

Name, said Maguire to himself, fumbling desperately for girls' names. "Van Kleef, sir," he blurted finally. "Maggi Van Kleef."

"Better get moving," said Stormcloud. As Maguire followed the little Indian across the field, the lieutenant called to Hanson. "Sergeant, is there a telephone in that control tower over there?"

"I believe there is, sir," said Hanson, who looked very grave and troubled.

"Lead on," said the lieutenant.

❖

"And so," said Maguire to the first sergeant, "with everybody's good and kind permission, I'll just fall by the dispensary and get that little matter taken care of."

"That sounds like a good idea," said Hanna.

"And then, if I could trouble you for a pass, I'll just run into San Fidel and clear up a few last-minute matters with the happy bride."

"That won't be necessary, Maguire," said the First. "The pass, I mean. The happy bride isn't in San Fidel. I took the trouble of looking her up in the phone book, and she's over at the regimental service club. I'll even walk you over."

"I really couldn't put you to the trouble!"

"No trouble at all," said Hanna. "Cooped up here in the orderly room, I could enjoy the walk."

Accustomed as he was to a brisk military pace, Sergeant Hanna found himself walking slower and slower to avoid leaving his companion behind.

"I really ought to go back," said Maguire, "and bathe and get into clean fatigues."

"You *are* nervous, aren't you?" said Hanna. "And absent-minded. You bathed and dressed up before you reported to the orderly room, remember?"

"I guess I *am* pretty flustered," Maguire said weakly.

❖

Out on Gehenna Boulevard, the dirt road in from the boondocks, the feet of Fox Company were churning up a prodigious amount of dust. The driver of a belated company truck could see the dust a mile ahead of him. Approaching the column, he could barely make out the figure of the rear Slow Man—the soldier who follows the column with a sign on his back to slow down oncoming motor traffic.

As he edged alongside the column the driver found the company commander barring his way. "Yes, sir!" said the driver, pulling to a stop. "How's it doing, sir?"

"Doing all right," said Jennison. "When you get to company, I've got a message for the first sergeant. He's supposed to have a bass drum meet us a mile out. Tell him to send the snare drum too." He rode the running board until the truck had reached the head of the column. Leaping off, he fell into step beside Little Beaver.

"Sir," said the Field First, "think we ought to give them a ten-minute break?"

"They look like they want it?" said the lieutenant.

"No, *sir!*" Stormcloud said emphatically. "I was just asking *you.*"

"Then to hell with the break," said Jennison. "Let's pick up the cadence."

"Third Platoon's got a new marching song," said Stormcloud. "It's real nice."

"If it's peppy, let's have it."

Stormcloud turned without losing step and signaled back to Hanson. "When the Roll!" he said.

"When the Roll!" said Hanson. Andy and Carleton took up the song; the others came in slowly, but soon they were all roaring it. The melody was an old gospel tune, "When the Roll Is Called Up Yonder," and the words went something like:

In a kindergarten classroom, as a little boy of three,
I was carefree, I was happy, till the day
That a hand reached in and grabbed me, and a voice said,
    "Come and see
What a lovely place we've found for you to play!"

We're so kind! kind! kind! to one another,
You will never even miss your home and mother!
There is candy, cake, and ice cream for the likes of
    you and me
In the dear old, sweet old U. S. Infantree!

Gliding in behind the chorus, the squad leaders eased through the intervening cadence—"Toop, thrip, fourp, HUP, toop, thrip"—and the platoon launched raucously into the second verse.

To the schoolrooms and the poolrooms and the hovels
    where we live,
From the cradle to the mortuary slab,
Comes a firm and friendly greeting from the Chief
    Executive:
Swap your rompers for a suit of olive drab!

Oh, we love! love! love! our friends and neighbors!
They appreciate our talents and our labors!
As a gesture of affection they've elected you and me
To the mean old, dirty old U. S. Infantree!

By this time some of the voices had begun sloughing off their inhibitions, noodling like a fife in and out and around the melody: diddle-dee oompadodda oompa, diddle-dee oompadodda ay. Lieutenant Jennison, grinning up ahead, decided they would have to try this one again when the drums met them.

Oh, the nation wants we all should grow up healthy,
    big, and strong,
For to function in a military way!
It's a real inspiring project, but it takes so very long
That the down upon our cheeks is turning gray!

We're too young and tender and delicate for the rigors
    of the service!
And harassment hurts our feelings, and the noise makes
    us nervous,

And there's many, oh many a place we'd rather spend
    our infancee
Than the mean old, dirty old U. S. Infantree!

The song over, they marched silently a while. Then the
company commander cut loose with a sigh. "Hot damn!" he
said to the field first sergeant. "That's a thigh-slapping doozer.
That's real military bitching. Where'd they pick it up?"

"It's home-grown, sir," said Stormcloud. "One of the men in
the Third Platoon made it up."

"Is that a fact?" said Lieutenant Jennison. "Who?"

"Private Sheaffer, sir. He's been a little loose in the head
ever since that day at the grenade pits."

❖

Maggi Van Kleef was sitting in the far corner of the service
club, flipping through a magazine and tapping her foot rather
ominously.

"I'll go over alone if I may," Maguire said to Sergeant Hanna.
"It's one of those moments when two's company."

"Okay," said Hanna.

"Here's a nice chair, close up front, and maybe I can find
you a copy of the *Army and Navy Journal*."

"Move out," said Hanna. "You shouldn't be thinking of me
at all at a time like this."

"I'll put something in the juke box for you," said Maguire.
Since it was a very loud juke box, he put fifty cents into it
and selected nothing but rock-and-roll recordings. Then he made
his way, slowly and tentatively, to the back corner where his
short-order fiancée sat stony-eyed and expectant. The smile he
threw her was shot down in midair.

"Hello, love bunny," he said hopefully.

"All right, Maguire," said Maggi, dispensing with the over-
ture. "Make it awfully good."

"Honey," he pleaded, "just for a mitzvah, smile at me just once—so that that sergeant back there can see it."

"I'm not impressing any sergeants," said Maggi.

"It's to save my life. I'm encircled by enemy snipers."

"Maguire," she said, "I haven't got the tiniest compulsion to save your life. You can save yourself time by taking the gas pipe."

"All right," he said forlornly. "No smile."

"I want you to talk real fast and real convincing," said Maggi. "I want to know just what kind of swindle you're working that drags me all the way out to Fort Burnside like this."

"Baby," said Maguire, "the last thing I would *ever* want—"

"In the middle of the afternoon," said Maggi, "I get a call from some first sergeant I never heard of, wanting to know if my *blood test* is in order! 'Blood test!' said I. 'To whom the hell do you think you are speaking?' "

"Boy!" said Maguire. "That's breaking it off in him!"

"He just wanted everything in order, he said! He didn't want anything to hold up the wedding! The wedding, Maguire! Your wedding and mine!"

"Lover," said Maguire, "you're hollering. Let's not televise the hearings. *Please* let's not." He laid a restraining hand on hers, and she flung it back at him.

"I want to know," she said, "what kind of rank little deal you're involved in that involves me. I want to know why, out of a clear blue, I'm engaged to *you*."

"It's all an unfortunate misunderstanding," said Maguire. "All I want is a chance to explain."

"Quit stalling for time," said Maggi. "You're not moving from this spot until you've explained."

"First," he said, "I'm an old man."

"Sure," she said, "with young ideas."

"Second," he said, "it was an eight-mile hike, with a full field pack, and I'm just not in condition. I'm out of training."

"Cut the flourishes," she said, "and take it from letter A."

He took it from A, but without cutting a single flourish.

"And that's how it was. To me it was just a hospital form, and I had no idea what was on it."

"And how did I get into it?"

"They asked me who, and yours was the name that sprang to my lips. The power of the subconscious. The power of my love for you."

He looked at her tenderly, wistfully, hopefully.

"Manure," said Maggi. "Rich, rotted horse manure!"

"I've told you that I love you," said Maguire. "I've hoped someday you would return that love. Spurn me if you must, but don't—don't scorn me, Maggi. That's more than I can stand."

"No conscience," she said, "no soul, no shame. Just a large stock of snake oil and a pocketful of labels."

"You're tearing the very heart out of me," said Maguire. "Beautiful and cruel. You're just not like yourself today."

"I don't know," said Maggi, grimly enjoying the situation. "I'm just wearing my hair different."

"What's to become of me, Maggi?"

"Keep groping around. Maybe you'll find the paddle again." She found a cigarette in her purse, lighted it, and gazed mockingly at him through the smoke. "Tell me," she said, "just for laughs. What did you expect me to do to pull you out of this?"

"Maggi," said Maguire, "will you marry me?"

"Thanks a lot," said Maggi, "but no thanks."

"Will you do one little thing for me?"

"Let's hear it."

"Will you break the engagement easily, gracefully?"

"Nope," she said. "I won't move a muscle. G.O., Maguire. Game's Over."

"Very well, Maggi," he said. "Nail me to the cross. I suppose it doesn't matter what I do now."

"If you want a friendly suggestion," said Maggi, "I'd advise you to leave town on the first thing smoking."

"Good-by, Maggi," he said, stooped with his infinite burden. He saw that she was rising, so he got to his own heavy feet.

"Good-by, old paint," said Maggi. She kissed him lightly, gaily, and walked away, leaving him hanging there.

"What's the trouble, old boy?" said the first sergeant as Maguire rejoined him. "You look like there's sickness in the family."

"Not my family," said Maguire, snatching at the cue. "It's *her* family. She wants to postpone the wedding."

"Well, put it off till *next* Saturday," said Hanna. "Then you've got two weeks' furlough you can use for a honeymoon. That's what *all* the lads in Fox Company are doing."

"Sure," said Maguire. "That's a grand little idea."

❖

With bass drum and snare, and the marching song they had practiced four times on the way in, the column turned into the company street. "Good Lord!" said Hanna, looking at his watch. He shot out to the veranda to watch them in.

Passing beneath the little porch, the company commander gave him a tired, weak, proud little grin, and the first sergeant winked back at him. Jennison marched the company all the way to the far end of the street, turned the column left and left again, and brought his men to a halt before the orderly room.

He conferred briefly with the first sergeant and turned back to them. "Men!" he said. "This unit is a bunch of ambelating fools. The time of the march—breaking all post records—is one hour and thirty-five minutes! Sergeant Hanna"—two hundred voices interrupted him with a roar, and then he finished the sentence—"take over!"

Elation swept the whole company that evening, missing only

one man: an owl-eyed private who paced back and forth in the Third Platoon latrine.

"I think he's really overshot himself this time," Hanna said to the company commander. "He played it pretty, but I don't think he's got the cards."

"We shall see what we shall see," Jennison said happily, "but I think you're acquiring a new eight-ball. Good thing too. Your old one, Sheaffer, seems to be wearing out."

❖

At the top of the company guidon staff, screwed like a lampshade between the staff and its ornamental tip, is a small inverted milk can painted infantry-blue and bearing a number in white. It is a different can each week, and a different number. The number designates the week of basic training through which the company is currently progressing, and thus it is an index to the minds and mood of the men ahead of whom the guidon travels.

This is what the numbers signify:

1. This is a group of some two hundred troubled, frightened, homesick boys, harried and bullied by their officers and noncoms and deeply resentful of them.

2. This group marches straighter and looks authority in the eye. It is astonished and pleased to find that all this military crud is not nearly as tough as it first appeared.

3. These young fellows know their way around. They have friends, and a certain knowledge of the military ropes, and they are neither frightened nor discouraged by what they are going through.

4. They are almost halfway through basic training, and halfway is over the hump.

5. These men have been home on leave, and been admired and fussed over, and given a chance at perspective. They have a sense of security that amounts almost to complacency.

6. To hell with it, say these men, there's only two weeks more to go. Cadremen may holler, but the trainees will take their own sweet time. They will not address their sergeant as "sir."

7. These are impatient, irritable, querulous men, and their bitching has an authentic military flavor. Why must time suddenly begin passing so slowly, and how can even military classes be this repetitious and boring?

8. There is little or nothing that can be done with these troops. They live only for Saturday morning, when the furlough papers will be passed out and this particular cycle will belong to the ages. Their thought is fervently shared by the cadre.

❖

It was on Monday evening of the eighth week that Private Andrew Sheaffer turned up in the orderly room, with his platoon sergeant's permission to see the first sergeant. Hanna was working late, preparing for the Organization Day rat race that was coming up on Thursday, and he welcomed the interruption.

"What the hell do you want?" he asked Andy. The latter took his abusive tone as a sure sign that the topkick was in a pleasant mood.

"Sergeant," he said, "I've been thinking things over, and I think I know now where I want to go for advanced training. The second eight weeks, that is."

"Well, I think that's just utterly delightful," said the first sergeant. "I'm happy for you. Where do you want to go? There's openings in a new school for barracks guards."

"I don't think I'd meet the qualifications for barracks guard," said Andy. "It's too confining."

"Day-room orderly, then?" said Hanna. "We need men of your caliber in that group."

"Too much responsibility," said Andy.

"All right, buster," said Hanna. "Where do you want to go?"

"If it's all the same to you," said Andy, "I'd like a crack at the Advanced Infantry School."

"Great God in the morning!" said the sergeant. "You? What on earth for?"

"Well, sir," said Andy, "it's kind of hard to explain. The way I figured it out, though, the Army didn't draft me to teach me a trade. I'm supposed to learn soldiering, not how to play a GI banjo. And I'm just teed-off enough at this whole military bit to want to whip it."

The first sergeant's face had no expression on it at all.

"I guess," said Andy, "I just want to see if I can do it. I want to see what the hell they can throw at me, and how I take it."

The sergeant was thoughtfully silent for a long time. "I must say," he said finally, "that's a mighty inspiring speech. Unfortunately, there's not a thing I can do for you. There's a little man in an ivory tower somewhere, and during your second week here you took some tests to send to him. That little man has studied those little tests to see what possibilities you had, if any. The Army has long past decided where you're going to go and what you're going to do."

"Do *you* know where I'm going?" said Andy.

"Sure," said Hanna. "I know everything there is to know in this company."

"Are you allowed to tell me where I'm going?"

"I sure as hell am."

"Well, *would* you tell me?"

"I sure as hell would. You and a bunch of others in this company, including your little friends Carleton and Maguire, were all-around dazzlers on the aptitude tests. You were golden boys in every category. Consequently, you boys are going to a special school." He paused and had trouble finding where he had put his cigarettes.

"What school?" said Andy, when he could stand it no more.

"Advanced Infantry School," said Hanna.

This time Andy was silent. He seemed to be carefully composing what he had to say, and when he spoke, he spoke slowly. "Sergeant," he said, "it's been a long, long time. Now it's almost the end of the trail. The time for good-bys."

"I'll be around the rest of the week. We'll probably run into each other."

"While I have this opportunity," said Andy, "I would like to say this. I've led a sheltered life, but I've also run into some real sons-of-bitches in my day. Never among them have I found such a sour, snide, double-dyed, self-propelled son-of-a-bitch as you, sergeant."

"Do go on," said Sergeant Hanna.

"From the minute I walked into this hen-house training company you've been on my back. You've done it in a nasty, sneaking little way, because the book doesn't allow you to do in the open what you've been doing behind the door. You've done your damnedest to eight-ball me for eight weeks, and I want to say thanks for the memories."

"You're perfectly welcome," said the sergeant.

"And I hope," Andy finished, "the next time I see you, you'll be broom sergeant in a company of Mongoloid idiots. Or a buck-bottom private in the same outfit as me."

"Is that all?" said the sergeant.

"That's all," said Andy. "That, and drop dead."

Sergeant Hanna grinned happily. "My, my, my," he said. "You're a very emotional boy."

Andy turned to leave, but as he neared the door a question occurred to him. "Where the hell is this Advanced Infantry School?"

"Oh, I thought you knew," said the topkick. "It's going to be Fox Company, Seventy-First United States Infantry, Fort Burnside, California."

Andy waited until he was sure that he had the use of his voice again. "Sergeant," he said, "you have a very strange look in your eye."

"It's not strange, son," said Hanna. "It's what they used to call a look of unholy glee. I've got great plans for you, boy."

❖

On Tuesday evening Andy Sheaffer became a soldier in reality. The melancholy Maguire was the first to learn about it; he came to throw himself upon his bunk, and beside him he saw Sheaffer, polishing his boots. "What are you doing that for?" Maguire asked him.

"Don't holler," said Andy. "Where's Hanson? Where's Henry Carleton?"

"They're nowhere around," said Maguire. "What are you doing?"

"I'm getting ready," said Andy, "to go a little ways over the hill. Sneak across A-wol Bridge and spend the evening with my baby."

"Which baby?" Maguire demanded suspiciously, resentfully.

"The real one," said Andy. "Not the one you've been trying to steal from me."

"Would you call the other one for me?" said Maguire. "She won't talk to me."

"Be realistic," said Andy. "You know what she'd say. She'd say, 'Speak for yourself, John. You're the one I really love.' It just wouldn't work, Maguire."

"I never knew I could hate anybody," said Maguire, "the way I hate you, Sheaffer."

"Why don't you sneak in yourself?" said Andy. "You're an old commuter on the A-wol Bridge."

"I think I will," said Maguire. Over the bridge they went, and down the gullies, and over the fence, and out.

In San Fidel they went their separate ways: Maguire to his hopeless campaigning, Sheaffer to a pleasant stolen evening with Little Sobersides.

Sobersides had not been expecting him, and when she opened the door and saw who it was she was overcome by a fit of the giggles.

"What's all this about?" said Andy.

"You!" said Susan. "You and your first sergeant! It isn't really true, is it?"

"What do you know about me and my first sergeant?" said Andy.

"What does the whole post know?" said Susan, trying to stop her laughter. "The whole community! The story's all over everywhere, Andy! My grandmother heard it from your colonel!"

"Oh, stop it," said Andy.

"It's a scream," said Susan. "And I'm so very proud of you, dear."

"I should think you would be," said Andy, beginning to feel quite pleased with himself. The two of them settled down together on a small portion of the end of the sofa. "At least," he said, "I know where I'm going to be for the next couple of months. Even with Hanna, that's something. There's going to be a lot of new faces, though. Practically everybody's shipping out somewhere. You know the funny thing, sweetie? I think practically every one of those eighteen-year-olds is planning to get married on his furlough."

"That's very admirable, probably," said Susan.

"Except me," said Andy. "And Carleton."

"And Maguire," said Susan. "I know all about that too."

"It's a wonderful institution," said Andy. "Marriage, that is."

"True," said Susan, not really impressed.

"I think," said Andy, "when two young people are old enough, and they know what they want, and they're ready to take on—" He stopped short. "What the hell are you laughing at now?"

"You!" said Susan. "You and that first sergeant! Andy, you're your old irresponsible self again!"

❖

He hitchhiked back to the post early, climbed the fence, scaled the gullies, crossed the bridge, and made his way back to Fox Company.

Maguire was sitting on the back steps, the picture of dejection and despair.

"How'd you make out?" said Andy.

"I stood there on a front porch most of the evening, banging on a front door and begging a girl to marry me. She laughed at me again." And, as a fraternal afterthought: "How'd you make out?"

"Practically the same," said Andy. "Word for word."

Hanson came out of the barracks and clicked his tongue at the two of them. "First sergeant knows you boys jumped the fence," he said. "I couldn't have covered up for you, even if I'd have wanted to."

"All right," said Maguire. "Let him do something to me."

"Don't go ape on me," said Hanson. "He's not going to take official cognizance of it. He says you're a sitting bird, and he's got other plans for Sheaffer."

"By George," said Andy, "that *is* big of him."

"The gideon-bearer fell off a ladder, and you're his replacement. Comes the big parade Thursday, you're going to be toting the banner."

"Me?" said Andy. "The guidon-bearer? That's a squad leader's job."

"Well, the first sergeant doesn't know that," said Hanson, "so suppose you just go ahead and do it anyway."

"Question, sergeant," said Maguire. "That's a real flashy job. Why should he give it to Sheaffer?"

"Well, the way he figures," said Hanson, "Fox Company is going to look so good in the review, we ought to give the other companies some kind of a handicap."

twelve

As SHRILL and fussy as Colonel Whippet was in his job of molding rookies into first-class fighting machines, the training in the Seventy-First could always go hang whenever the occasion arose for a ceremonial whing-ding. Colonel Whippet loved to see flags flying and the whole regiment marching to the brassy blare of his horrible little regimental band. He could have watched this sort of thing all day long. It was good for the men, he said; it gave them esprit de corps and a Sense of Tradition. Regardless of what it did for the troops, it unquestionably had this effect upon the regimental commander, and he was the one who counted.

Organization Day, like Christmas, came but once a year, and this was Organization Day. The colonel's face was mellow and proud. His hopelessly romantic heart overflowed with emotion, and there was a catch in his voice as he stood there on the reviewing stand—surrounded by the regimental relatives, the neighborhood dignitaries, the regimental sweetheart (a grotesquely pneumatic blonde from one of the best families in La Salada), and every officer of his command—and bestowed upon thirty outstanding young trainees the red and white ribbon of the Good Conduct Medal.

A Mrs. Arthur Sheaffer, a regimental relative in the stands, turned to the bald and beaming gentleman beside her. "Arthur," she said, "why are they getting medals?"

"Because, my dear," said Mr. Sheaffer, "they are the ones who've been behaving themselves."

When the thirtieth young hand had been fervently clasped and unclasped, Colonel Whippet pulled out several more stops, including the diapason, and went on to what he described as the happiest occasion of the day. The company that had received the most points in the past four months—for superlative administration, supply, drill, mess, and maintenance of barracks, day room, and game room—was now to receive the regimental trophy as the best company in the Seventy-First United States Infantry.

"This trophy, as you know, has hung for two years in the orderly room of Fox Company, despite the valiant efforts of other companies to wrest it from them. The regiment will be happy to know that this year the regimental trophy has been awarded to"—he paused, looked all about him, and smiled— "Fox Company of the Seventy-First!"

First Lieutenant Jesse L. Jennison, ramrod-stiff and extremely self-conscious, made his way to the colonel's point, accepted the trophy and the hearty handshake, and lugged his familiar prize back to his seat. He leaned the three-foot plaque against the chair, making a wall between himself and the company sweetheart, a vivacious young heifer from Smithville.

The regimental troops, arrayed across the field in thirteen company formations, did not cheer the victory, because no one had told them to. Massed behind their "officers"—battalion sergeants major, first sergeants, and platoon sergeants—they stood stolidly, absorbing esprit and tradition and hoping that none of their number would goof.

A gaudily polished jeep pulled up to the reviewing stand, and the regimental commander handed the regimental sweetheart into it. The jeep darted out to the center of the field to pick up the commander of troops, who on more realistic occasions was the regimental sergeant major. The commander of troops climbed ponderously into the jeep, and the little reviewing party "trooped the line," making a full circuit around the formation. When this was finished, and the dignitaries had resumed their places on the stand, and the jeep had been disposed of, the regimental sergeant major stood alone, his beefy back turned to the stands. "Pass in review!" he roared, as if this were his full-time job. The regimental band sounded off and moved out, the thirteen companies falling in behind it.

"They're going away!" said Madeline.

"They're coming back," said Susan Daniel, who was sitting on the other side of Arthur.

"They've got to get a good start," said Arthur, "down at the far end of the field."

The brave, uncertain little band aimed itself at them again and came past the reviewing point. Five companies passed them in impressive formation, twelve ranks across and fourteen deep, and went largely unnoticed. Fox Company came into view, and Susan pointed it out, and Madeline bounced up and down and gave excited little squeals.

It was a well-drilled company, precise and sure. Six paces ahead of it, in the stead of the company commander, marched the prim, upright, resplendent figure of its first sergeant. Two paces behind him, and one step to either side, were two figures hardly less dazzling. Behind him on the near side was the company bugler, his bugle braced against his right hip, its tasseled blue silk banner fluttering against his arm. Beside and beyond the bugler marched another soldier with a large pale blue banner on a tall pole. The pole somewhat obscured his face.

Madeline scanned the front row of soldiers—platoon sergeants and guides—and found no Andy there. She searched as best she could among the second rank—squad leaders—and decided that her son was being hidden from her.

"There!" said Susan. "In front!"

"Eyes right!" barked the first sergeant as the formation drew nearer. Madeline's own eyes were caught by the guidon as it descended to the horizontal, and then she saw the bearer's face as it turned straight toward her.

"It's Andy!" she said. "It is! Oh, isn't he *beautiful?*"

"He's just ravishing," said Susan.

Arthur's comment was slower in coming. "My dear," he said, "this is the kind of school we should have sent him to ten years ago."

The formation moved past, the beatific vision was gone, and so was Madeline Sheaffer's interest in the remainder of the review.

"There's one thing I don't like," she said. "First he's a waiter, then he's a servant to the colonel, and now he has to carry that heavy pole."

"What's wrong with that?" said Arthur.

"It just seems to me," said Madeline, "they go out of their way to give him all the menial jobs."

"It could be worse," said Arthur. "Suppose they made him wear those heavy, ugly stripes like the sergeants wear?"

"They wouldn't dare," said Madeline.

"You're probably right, my dear," said Arthur. "They wouldn't dare."

❖

After the luncheon in the company mess there was a field meet in the post stadium. Arthur Sheaffer restively watched the three-legged races and the pie-eating contests, and when the main attraction was announced—a tug-of-war between the company commanders and the first sergeants—he announced that he had had enough.

"The conclusion is foregone," he said to the rest of his group. "The first sergeants will win by sheer weight of weight. It is my intention to get out of here and stretch my legs."

"Very well, Arthur," said his wife. "By all means, be rude."

"May I have the company of my son to pace me?"

"You may," she said. "Go pace him, Andrew."

Past the meaningless accumulation of tanks, machine guns, bazookas, mortars, and reckless rifles, Arthur took his son's arm in an almost Parisian fashion. They strolled along, enjoying the comparative quiet.

"You're looking marvelously well, Andrew," said Arthur. "As alert and intelligent as you looked at twelve. I suspect you're feeling good, as well."

"Funny thing, father," said Andrew. "I think I am. It's not my way of life, but I'm learning to lean into it."

"Do you like it here?"

"I think I could learn to," said Andy. "Enough, at least."

"I was speaking to that top sergeant of yours," said Arthur. "Sergeant What's-his-name."

"Sergeant Hanna," said Andy.

"I suppose you call him Hard-Hearted Hanna?" said Arthur.

Andy grinned at him. "They would have in your day," he said. "Not any more. That type of gag is classed as pure succotash these days."

"That's good," said Arthur. "He seems a very high type of noncommissioned officer, and a very nice person too."

"He might very well be," said Andy. "I'm not in a position to know."

"He has a gratifyingly healthy regard for you."

"Healthy," said Andy, "is the kind of regard I have for him too."

"How are you and Susan working out?"

"I'm going to marry her."

"That's very nice," said Arthur. "Does she know?"

"Not yet."

"The sooner she knows," said Arthur, "the better. Andrew, I have something to say that might astonish you. I hardly know how to begin."

"Take your time," said Andy.

"I am attaining a disturbingly ripe old age," said Arthur, "and I have to think of my future. When you finish with the Army, or it finishes with you, I'd like you to consider coming to work for me."

"For you?" said Andy. "That *is* astonishing."

"I think you'd like the publishing business," said Arthur. "It's not a wealthy business, but it's pleasant and even respectable if you do it right. I don't suppose you'd ever consider it."

"As a matter of fact," said Andy, "I think it's a wonderful business. And I think you'd make a reasonably nice employer."

"Strange," said Arthur. "I never suspected you had any interest in it at all."

"I could have told you," said Andy, "except that you never asked."

"Is it a deal?" said Arthur.

"It's a deal," said Andy. "Shake."

"Don't say anything to your mother," said Arthur. "I'm not at all sure she'd approve."

❖

Suddenly it was Saturday, and the whole thing was over. The bedding had been turned in, the mattresses left on the bunks and rolled into S shapes, which, in a couple of weeks, newcomers to the company would be unfolding. The baggage had all been stacked between the barracks, and the buildings themselves had been cleaned and inspected and locked—all except the barracks down at the end of the row, the one where the leftover men would be staying.

There was a carefree gaiety in the company street today. The formations were almost no formations at all, because nobody really cared on this particular Saturday morning. "Column of bunches!" was Sergeant Stormcloud's order. "Strawberry-pickers to the left!" Finally, it seemed, everybody fell into a milling herd clustered about the orderly-room veranda.

Sergeant Hanna sat on a chair on the veranda—it was the first time that any of them had ever seen a chair there—and leafed through a pile of papers in front of him. These were the orders. On the steps beneath him sat Pfc Polier with another stack of papers, each of them worth thirteen days' leave to the man whose name it bore.

"As I call your name," the sergeant shouted, "sound off and step right up!" He looked out over the crowd. "What the hell are you skulking around for, Maguire? I got nothing with your name on it."

"Chaplain's been calling for him," said Polier.

"Chaplain's been calling for you, Maguire!" said Sergeant Hanna. "Get your behind over to the chapel—on the double!"

Maguire shook hands with some of the men he would not be seeing again, and then the saddening thought swept over him that, for all he knew, he would never be seeing any of them again. This was the morning of doom.

He patted his pockets into shape, and wiped a boot top on the blouse of his trousers, and started the suddenly all-too-short hike to the Protestant chapel. All that he could do was to explain, to apologize, and to die.

He went up the steps and opened the door. He dragged himself past the rack of religious tracts, waited long seconds before the office door, and then knocked—very, very softly.

"Come in!" boomed the chaplain's cheery voice, and the condemned man pushed open the door.

Behind his desk sat Chaplain Russell. Beside it, at that instant turning toward him, was the last person on earth he ever expected to find there. Maguire's shoulders went up, his eyes regained their luster, and the man himself was born anew— a creature of vigor and confidence and galvanized crust.

"Good morning, sir!" he caroled. "And good morning, my love! I hope I didn't keep anyone waiting!"

❖

"I'm sure you young people will excuse me," the chaplain said archly. "I have a few chores outside, and you'll want to sit and visit for a while."

He crept out of the room, closing the door with elaborate slowness and quiet, and the two of them stood facing each other.

"Somewhere," said Maggi, straining to cover the awkward silence, "he's got the idea I just flew down from Oregon."

"Maggi," said Ransom, "you're the most beautiful sight I ever saw."

"I can well imagine," said Maggi, the smile coming back.

"I'm speechless," said Maguire. "I just can't believe it."

"Can't you, now?" said Maggi. "Then get that little egg-sucking grin off your face. You look like a cat reaching into a bird cage."

"I never even dreamed that *you*'d be here."

"Why shouldn't I be here? It's my wedding day. I'm curious to see how you're going to make an honest woman of me."

"Don't be flip," said Maguire. "Don't joke around. This is a very solemn occasion."

"Is it, Maguire?" said Maggi.

"Honey," said Maguire, "you know it."

"It jolly well better be," she said, coming to him and taking his shoulders in her hands. "You've got a job cut out for you, Jack. From here out, you either fish or cut bait."

"Upon my sacred word of honor—"

"No promises," said Maggi. "Just toe my line and I'll toe yours."

"I love you," said Maguire.

"I love you," said Maggi.

"Since when?" said Maguire.

"Since about the third time you came prowling around, with your horrible line of corn and your larcenous heart on your sleeve."

"You gave me an awfully hard time this week," he said.

"Didn't I though? Well, that's only a sample, Maguire. Keep one foot on the base, or I'll tag you out every time. When Mamma's around, you're not playing the local sandlot boys; you're in the big leagues."

"Honey," he said, "I'm going to be a changed man."

"You're not just whistling Dixie," said Maggi.

Maguire kissed her somewhat reverently, and then suddenly sat down, almost pulling her with him.

"What is it?" said Maggi.

"Conscience," said Maguire. "Andy Sheaffer. My best friend. What have I done to *him?*"

"You've delivered him," said Maggi, "right into the hands of the dull girl who was made for him."

"It's very awkward," said Maguire. "What can I say to him?"

"Well, think about it," said Maggi. "He'll be here in another twenty minutes."

"Why?"

"I thought you'd like him for your best man. He came all the way into town to bring me out this morning. Now he's gone back for a bridesmaid."

"The Daniel girl?"

"Who else?" said Maggi. "He wants to get her in the mood."

"Maggi Van Kleef," said Maguire, "Maggi Maguire to be, you're a shrewd, shrewd woman."

"I have to be," said Maggi, "in the company I travel with."

❖

From the moment that Chaplain Russell came back into his little office until the moment that he invited the bridegroom to kiss the bride there was a hectic lapse of some thirteen hours. It was that rare sort of day that always made the chaplain happy.

First it was discovered that Private Maguire, after all the fuss about it, still had not had his blood test. Since this was not only a Saturday but a holiday as well, it looked as if he would not get it. Chaplain Russell called the blood clinic at the hospital. "The boy *must* get it," he firmly told the captain on the other end of the line. "We can't have an unmarried girl stranded at Fort Burnside over the weekend." The captain agreed to process the blood that morning.

The wedding party forgathered again in the chapel at three that afternoon. The bridegroom-elect had all the papers that were required of him, including a copy of his divorce decree. The bride-elect was not so well equipped. Somewhere in the rush it had slipped her mind that she too needed a blood-test certificate.

At this point the bride-elect dissolved in nervous tears. She was comforted by her maid of honor while the chaplain got on the telephone again.

The bridegroom-elect's witness, Private Sheaffer, repeatedly importuned the happy man to stop pacing and fidgeting. "It's not the last day of the world," he said. "You could even get married on Tuesday."

"If you can't be helpful," said Private Maguire, "just shut

up, will you? You heard what the chaplain said about strand-
ing unmarried girls."

None of the doctors on Chaplain Russell's list were at the
moment equipped to administer the test; everything was closed
up for the weekend.

At four o'clock there was a telephone call from a Mrs.
Randolph in the license bureau at Esperanza. "Chaplain," she
said, "shall we call it a day? I'm not even supposed to be
open now!"

"Just stay there and hold your horses," said the chaplain.
"We'll be there in no time at all."

At four-twenty the reverend major located an Army laboratory that happened to be processing blood for some other,
probably unromantic, purpose. "What's the rush?" the laboratory asked. "The girl pregnant or something?"

Struck by inspiration, but unwilling to lie, the chaplain
merely said, "It's none of your business."

"All right, sir," said the laboratory. "Get her over here."

At eight that evening the chaplain took a breather for himself by uniting another young couple in the bonds of holy
wedlock. The Van Kleef-Maguire party watched the ceremony
wistfully from a rear pew.

At nine the laboratory called to say that the tests were completed and the papers could be picked up.

"We'll take my car," said the chaplain, scorning the MG
and Maguire's neat new coupé. "It's old, but it's roomy enough
for all of us."

From the laboratory they raced across the boondock to
Esperanza, where Mrs. Randolph was still waiting in the license
bureau. The license finally granted, they raced back to Fort
Burnside and the chapel. Sergeant Hanson was sitting on the
steps, waiting for them.

By eleven o'clock they were ready for the ceremony.

"My assistant has sneaked out somewhere," said the chaplain. "Can anyone play the organ?"

"I play the piano," said Private Sheaffer. "Maybe I could figure it out."

"Up to the loft, then," said the chaplain. "There's something rushed and sordid about a marriage without music."

Private Maguire stood alone and nervous at the altar. From the loft there came, in wavering and uncertain tones, the lardy strains of the Wagner wedding march. The bride-elect came down the aisle on Hanson's arm. The organist rushed down the stairs and took his place beside the bridegroom.

A few minutes later the whole thing was over.

Somewhere, somehow, in that busy day, the chaplain had found reservations for the bridal pair at a place called the Welcome Travelers Motel. They had not the heart to tell him that they already had a place to go.

He stood on the porch of the chapel, fondly waving them farewell, and then he turned to the others: Andy, Susan, and Sergeant Hanson.

"There, now," he said. "I'm just getting my second wind. Any other takers?"

He turned his sharpest glance on Susan, who was sniffling into a handkerchief.

"Thank you," she said. "I'd need a few days to think it over."

"Yes," said the chaplain, "and to get all the papers in order."

thirteen

ONE OF THE NEW men in the First Platoon's downstairs squad room looked at the next man and rolled his eyes. "From the looks of the cadre around here, this outfit is going to be worse than the last."

"It looks real hen-house," said the second man. "And this Hollywood sergeant looks like their secret weapon."

The cadreman in the blue pot and the brassard of an acting sergeant strode heavily toward the center of the room. A third of the way down the squad-room aisle he dropped his cigarette into a butt can and put both his hands on his hips. "All right, you men," he said. "Let's stop potskying around and give me your attention. Let's make like a little cluster around me."

They gathered around, and the acting sergeant put one highly polished boot on the foot of the nearest bunk. His cold eyes wandered about the group until they found a man who seemed a little too relaxed.

"All right, soldier," said the sergeant. "If you want to lie down, you go and get the sick book first.

"Now, if I have the rest of you people's attention. You men are now members of the First Platoon, Fox Company, Seventy-First United States Infantry. You're in the best platoon of the best company of the best regiment in the whole Army, and I'm here to see that you keep it that way.

"My name is Sergeant Sheaffer, and I'm you lucky people's platoon sergeant for your advanced infantry training. For the next eight weeks I'm supposed to be a mother and a father to you, whether you like it or not. I'm a hard man but a fair one, and there's no sweat getting along with me if you want to. If you do right, we'll be real tight. If you screw it up, your behinds are grass, and Sergeant Sheaffer is the lawnmower.

"Private Maguire here has been in my platoon. He can tell you what it's like."

"He's a hard man," spoke up Private Maguire. "But fair."

"You people have all been through basic training," said the sergeant, "so you can't plead ignorance any more. Having finished basic, you are here to learn how to be a soldier. You're going to have it hard and heavy, and you're going to learn a lot of things your mothers never taught you—signal communications, the automatic rifle, the sixty-millimeter mortar, the light machine gun, and the fifty-seven-millimeter reckless rifle. You're going to learn about the squad and the rifle platoon, the infantry tank team, and a lot of other things you never knew existed.

"The first thing you're going to learn, though, is how to make your bed Fox Company fashion. You're going to learn that from Corporal Carleton here, who's an expert in that field."

The group turned as one to inspect the corporal: a sharp, capable-looking Negro lad with a trace of amusement in his eyes. The twinkle, strangely, made him seem a dangerous man to fool with.

"Now let's get several things straight before we start," said Sergeant Sheaffer. "You heard what the first sergeant said about shipshape and Bristol-fashion. It might help you to know that, beside Sergeant Hanna, I myself am a holy terror on this point. I want these barracks to stand tall at all times. If not, they will chew me and I will chew you, for this is the Law of the Jungle. Is that clear?"

"That's clear, sergeant!" said several well-trained voices.

"I want the men of this platoon to stand tall also. I want

you to get up in the morning bright-eyed and bushy-tailed, and I want you to go through the day eager to excel. Leave your pockets unbuttoned, and I will cut the buttons off for you. Put your hands in them, and I will fill them with sand. I want no daydreaming; I want no goofing. When I say, 'Jump!' all I want to hear from you is, 'How high?' "

There was a faint razzing sound at the far edge of the group, and Sergeant Sheaffer's eyes sought out the man. "Soldier," he said, "it's my policy to give a dog and a damned fool one chance. You have just had yours."

The group stood lost in thoughtful silence.

"The last thing any of you people want to do," the platoon sergeant concluded, "is to irritate me. You want to make me happy at all times. This is to be your main purpose in life. Any questions?"

There were no questions.

"All right, corporal," he said to the sharp young Negro cadreman beside him, "take over!" And he walked out of the room with a faintly terrifying swagger.

❖

The first sergeant was standing on the orderly-room porch as Andy went past. "Once a bug-out, always a bug-out," said Hanna. "Where are you off to this time?"

"I'll tell you, sergeant," said Andy. "It's such a nice crisp evening, I thought I'd go for a stroll."

"When you get to the head of the street, sergeant," said Hanna, "do me a favor. Go for a ride instead. That damned little car of yours is blocking the street again, and the girl in it is distracting the troops."

"You're old and sour," said Andy, "and you've got no romance in you."

"That's the Lord's truth," said Hanna. "If that was *my* girl I'd pop the question to her and get it over with. Getting married is the best cure for a case of young love. Do me a favor. Go ahead and ask her."

"Ask her, nothing," said Andy. "Tonight I'm going to tell her."

"That's the Army way," said Hanna. "A firm, quiet tone of command."

❖

Susan finally broke away from the kiss. "Andy," she said, "really! We're practically in your company street. And it's full of people."

"They've seen soldiers before," said Andy. He came around the front of the MG and got in beside her. "And furthermore, I'll do the thinking around here."

"Were you impressive?" she said. "Frightening? What did you say to those poor boys?"

Andy told her, almost word for word.

"It almost frightens *me*," said Susan, "and I know what a mushhead you are. You're a softie."

"I'm a hard man," said Andy, "but fair."

"Let's get away from here," said Susan.

"First," he said, "we're going to have a brief orientation. We're going over some of the gaps in your training chart. I am highly displeased with your marital status."

"Yes, sir," said Susan.

"And the last thing you want to do," said Andy, "is to irritate me. You want to make me happy."

"That's my main purpose in life," said Susan.

"Next Saturday?"

"That's too quick!" she wailed. "We don't have to have a GI wedding. You can carry this military stuff too far, you know."

"All right," said Andy. "The Saturday after."

"That's an order?"

"A direct order."

"Yes, sir," she said contentedly. "Now may I drive us somewhere where it's lonely and dark?"

"That's an order too," said Andy.

"Boy!" said Susan. "Is *this* a gung-ho outfit!"

❖

From the journals of Private Maguire, E-2:

329. Its these young oficious ones that are the worst. Sample dialogue from Sgt. Sheaffer to oldest and dearest friend: "Dont start riding the sick book on *me*, Maguire. If your sick, go on sick call. If your not sick, thats a good way to get sick." This babe hes marrying will take a lot of that military guff out of him. Always watch the quiet ones.

330. A 368 is Army regulation 615-368. Extends benefits of discharge to enlisted men who demonstrate they are antisocial, amorral, alcoholic, patho. liar, repeated petty offenses or a Habitual Shirker. God knows I am eligible, but Mrs. Maguire will not hear of it.

331. Only alternative for man who is old, tired, and just no Dam good as a soldier. Officer Candidate School. Check further.

Dam the torpedoes. Full speed ahead.